among the brave

among the brave

the

brave

A Shadow Children Book

MARGARET
PETERSON
HADDIX

SCHOLASTIC INC.

New York Toronto London Auckland Sydney
Mexico City New Delhi Hong Kong Buenos Aires

No part of this publication may be reproduced, or stored in a retrieval system, or transmitted in any form or by any means, electronic, mechanical, photocopying, recording, or otherwise, without written permission of the publisher. For information regarding permission, write to Simon & Schuster Books for Young Readers, Simon & Schuster Children's Publishing Division, 1230 Avenue of the Americas, New York, NY 10020.

ISBN 0-439-67135-3

12 11 10 9 8 7 6 5 4 3 2 1   4 5 6 7 8 9/0

Printed in the U.S.A.   23

First Scholastic printing, September 2004

Book design by Greg Stadnyk
The text for this book is set in Elysium.

For Jeff

With thanks to Gillian McIntosh, John Peterson, and Mary Fleming for their assistance with this book.

CHAPTER ONE

G reat, Trey thought. *I do one brave thing in my entire life, and now it's like, 'Got anything dangerous to do? Send Trey. He can handle it.' Doesn't anyone remember that Cowardice is my middle name?*

Actually, only two other people in the entire world had ever known Trey's real name, and one of them was dead. But Trey didn't have time to think about that. He had a crisis on his hands. He'd just seen two people killed, and others in danger. Maybe he'd been in danger too. Maybe he still was. He and his friends had left the scene of all that death and destruction and total confusion, jumped into a car with an absolute stranger, and rushed off in search of help. They'd driven all night, and now the car had stopped in front of a strange house in a strange place Trey had never been before.

And Trey's friends actually expected him to take control of the situation.

"What are you waiting for?" his friend Nina asked. "Just go knock on the door."

"Why don't you?" Trey asked, which was as good as admitting that he wasn't as brave as a girl. No courage, no pride. Translate that into Latin and it'd be a good personal motto for him. *Nulla fortitudo nulla superbia,* maybe? Trey allowed himself a moment to drift into nostalgia for the days when his biggest challenges had been figuring out how to translate Latin phrases.

"Because," Nina said. "You know. Mr. Talbot and I—well, let's just say I've got a lot of bad memories."

"Oh," Trey said. And, if he could manage to turn down his fear a notch or two, he did understand. Mr. Talbot, the man they had come to see, had once put Nina through an extreme test of her loyalties. It had been necessary, everyone agreed—even Nina said so. But it hadn't been pleasant. Mr. Talbot had kept her in prison; he'd threatened her with death.

Trey was glad he'd never been put through a test like that. He knew: He'd fail.

Trey glanced up again at the hulking monstrosity of a house where Mr. Talbot lived. He wasn't dangerous, Trey reminded himself. Mr. Talbot was going to be their salvation. Trey and Nina and a few of their other friends had come to Mr. Talbot's so they could dump all their bad news and confusion on him. So he would handle everything, and they wouldn't have to.

Trey peered toward the front of the car, where his friends Joel and John sat with the driver. Or, technically, the "chauffeur," a word derived from the French. Only the

M A R G A R E T   P E T E R S O N   H A D D I X

original French word—*chauffer?*—didn't mean "to drive." It meant "to warm" or "to heat" or something like that, because chauffeurs used to drive steam automobiles.

Not that it mattered. Why was he wasting time thinking about foreign verbs? Knowing French wasn't going to help Trey in the least right now. It couldn't tell him, for example, whether he could trust the driver. Everything would be so easy if he could know, just from one word, whether he could send the driver to knock on Mr. Talbot's door while Trey safely cowered in the car.

Or how about Joel or John? Granted, they were younger than Trey, and maybe even bigger cowards. They'd *never* done anything brave. Still—

"Trey?" Nina said. *"Go!"*

She reached around him and jerked open the door. Then she gave him a little shove on the back, so suddenly that he was surprised to find himself outside the car, standing on his own two feet.

Nina shut the door behind him.

Trey took a deep breath. He started to clench his fists out of habit and fear—a habit of fear, a fear-filled habit— and only stopped when pain reminded him that he was still clutching the sheaf of papers he'd taken from a dead man's desk. He glanced down and saw a thin line of fresh blood, stark and frightening on the bright white paper.

Trey's next breath was sharp and panicked. Had someone shot him? Was he in even greater danger than he'd imagined? His ears buzzed, and he thought he might pass out from terror. But nothing else happened, and after a few moments his mind cleared a little.

He looked at the blood again. It was barely more than a single drop.

Okay, Trey steadied himself. *You just had a panic attack over a paper cut. Let's not be telling anybody about that, all right?*

A paper cut indoors would have been no big deal. But outdoors—outdoors, the need to *breathe* was enough to panic him.

He forced himself to breathe anyway. And, by sheer dint of will, Trey made himself take a single step forward. And then another. And another.

Mr. Talbot had a long, long walkway between the street and his house, and the chauffeur had inconveniently parked off to the side, under a clump of trees that practically hid the car from the house. Trey considered turning around, getting back into the car, and telling the chauffeur to pull up closer—say, onto the Talbots' front porch. But that would mean retracing his steps, and Trey felt like he'd already come so far.

Maybe even all of three feet.

With part of his mind, Trey knew he was being foolish—a total baby, a chicken, a fear-addled idiot.

It's not my fault, Trey defended himself. *It's all . . . conditioning. I can't help the way I was raised.* And that was the understatement of the year. For most of his thirteen years, Trey hadn't had control over any aspect of his life.

He was an illegal third child—the entire Government thought he had no right to exist. So he'd had to hide, from birth until age twelve, in a single room. And then, when he was almost thirteen, when his father died . . .

You don't have time to think about that now, Trey told himself sternly. *Walk.*

He took a few more steps forward, propelled now by a burning anger that he'd never managed to escape. His mind slipped back to a multiple-choice test question he'd been asking himself for more than a year: *Whom do you hate? A) Him; B) Her; C) Yourself?* It never worked to add extra choices: *(D) All of the above; E) A and B; F) A and C; or G) B and C?* Because then the question just became, *Whom do you hate the most?*

Stop it! Trey commanded himself. *Just pretend you're Lee.*

Trey's friend Lee had been an illegal third child like Trey, but Lee had grown up out in the country, on an isolated farm, so he'd been able to spend plenty of time outdoors. He'd almost, Trey thought, grown up normal. As much as Trey feared and hated being outdoors, Lee craved it.

"How can you stand it?" Trey had asked Lee once. "Why aren't you terrified? Don't you ever think about the danger?"

"I guess not," Lee had said, shrugging. "When I'm outdoors I look at the sky and the grass and the trees, and I guess that's all I think about."

Trey looked at the sky and the grass and the trees around him, and all he could think was, *Lee should be here, walking up to Mr. Talbot's door, instead of me.* Lee had been in the car with Trey and Nina and Joel and John until just about ten minutes earlier. But Lee had had the chauffeur drop him and another boy, Smits, off at a cross-roads in the middle of nowhere because, Lee had said, "I have to get Smits to safety."

Trey suspected that Lee was taking Smits home, to Lee's parents' house, but Trey was trying very hard not to think that. It was too dangerous. Even thinking about it was dangerous.

And thinking about it made Trey jealous, because Lee still had a home he could go to, and parents who loved him, and Trey didn't.

But Lee would be dead right now if it weren't for me, Trey thought with a strange emotion he barely recognized well enough to name. Pride. He felt proud. And, cowardly Latin motto or no, he had a right to that pride.

For Trey's act of bravery—his only one ever—had been to save Lee's life the night before.

Beneath the pride was a whole jumble of emotions Trey hadn't had time to explore. He felt his leg muscles tense, as if they too remembered last night, remembered springing forward at the last minute to knock Lee to the side, only seconds before the explosion of glass in the very spot where Lee had stood. . . .

It's easier being brave when you don't have time to think about your other options, Trey thought. *Unlike now.*

He had so many choices, out here in the open. The ones

that called to him most strongly were the ones that involved hiding. How fast would he be able to run back to the car, if he needed to? Would the clump of trees be a good hiding place? Would he be able to squeeze out of sight between that giant flowerpot on the porch and the wall of the Talbot house?

Trey forced himself to keep walking. It seemed a miracle when he finally reached the front porch. He cast a longing glance toward the flowerpot, but willed himself to stab a finger at the doorbell.

Dimly, he could hear a somber version of "Westminster Chimes" echoing from indoors. Nobody came. He took a second to admire the brass door knocker, elegantly engraved with the words, GEORGE A. TALBOT, ESQUIRE. Still nobody came.

Too bad, Trey thought. *Back to the car, then.* But his legs didn't obey. He couldn't face the thought of walking back through all that open space again. He pressed the doorbell again.

This time the door opened.

Trey was torn between relief and panic. Relief won when he saw Mr. Talbot's familiar face on the other side of the door. *See, this wasn't so bad,* Trey told himself. *I walked all the way up here without my legs even trembling. Take that, Nina! I am braver than you!*

Trey started thinking about what he was supposed to say to Mr. Talbot. He hadn't worried about that before. Words were so much easier than action.

"I'm so glad you're home, Mr. Talbot," Trey began. "You won't believe what happened. We just—"

But Mr. Talbot cut him off.

"No, no, I do not want to buy anything to support your school's lacrosse team," he said. "And please do *not* come back. Tell the rest of your team that this is a no-soliciting house. Can't you see I'm a busy man?"

Mr. Talbot's eyebrows beetled together, like forbidding punctuation.

"But, Mr. Talbot—I'm not—I'm—"

Too late. The door slammed in his face.

"—Trey," Trey finished in a whisper, talking now to the door.

He doesn't remember me, Trey thought. It wasn't that surprising. Every time Mr. Talbot had visited Hendricks School, where Trey and Lee were students, Trey had been in the background, no more noticeable than the wallpaper.

Lee, on the other hand, had been front and center, talking to Mr. Talbot, joking with him, going off for special meals with him.

Mr. Talbot wouldn't have slammed the door in Lee's face, Trey thought. Was Trey jealous of that, too? *No. I just wish Lee were here to talk with Mr. Talbot now.*

Trey sighed, and began gathering the nerve to ring the doorbell again.

But then two things happened, one after the other.

First, a car shot out from under the house—from a hidden garage, Trey guessed. It was black and long and official-looking. Its tires screeched, winding around the curves of the driveway. Trey caught a glimpse of two men in uniforms in the front seat, and Mr. Talbot in the back. Mr. Talbot held up his hands toward the window, toward Trey, and Trey saw a glint of something metal around his wrists.

Handcuffs?

The black car bounced over the curb and then sped off down the street.

Trey was still standing there, his mouth agape, his mind struggling to make sense of what he'd seen, when the car he'd ridden in—the car that Nina, Joel, and John were still hiding in—began to inch forward, under the cover of the trees. Trey felt a second of hope: *They're coming to rescue me!*

But the car was going in the wrong direction.

Trey stared as the car slid away, just a shadow in the trees, then a black streak on the open road.

Then it was gone.

They left me! Trey's mind screamed. *They left me!*

He was all alone on an uncaring man's porch—an arrested man's porch?—out in the great wide open where anyone in the world might see him.

Without thinking, Trey dived behind the huge flower-pot, to hide.

CHAPTER *TWO*

For once, Trey's instincts had been wise. Seconds later, a whole army of black cars swarmed down the street and onto the Talbots' property. They overflowed the drive-way; the last few cars had to park harum-scarum on the lawn. Peeking daringly over the rim of the huge flowerpot, Trey saw the doors of all the cars opening, and dozens of men in black uniforms spilling out. He ducked down immediately, trying to fit his body in as small a space as possible behind the flowerpot.

You know, it really wasn't a good idea to grow four inches in the past year, he thought, then marveled that he could think so clearly at a time like this. He pulled his long legs even closer to his body.

Walkie-talkies crackled instructions: "Search the base-ment."

"Affirmative."

"Search the yard."

Trey began to sweat. What if someone was dispatched

MARGARET PETERSON HADDIX

to search the porch? He strained to hear every instruction, all at once. He listened for footsteps up to the porch. It wouldn't take any great observational skills to find Trey. What was he going to do if—no, when—that happened?

Come out fighting, Trey ordered himself sternly. *Don't go down gently. You'll have the element of surprise on your side. As soon as you hear someone nearby, jump up and start swinging punches. . . .*

And then what? Did he really think he could prevail? Maybe he could surprise one of the uniformed men. Temporarily. But two? Three? Fifty?

A board creaked nearby. The first step of the stairs up to the porch had creaked just like that when Trey was walking to the door. His heart began pounding so hard he thought the sound itself would give him away. He held his breath as another board creaked, and then another. Closer, closer . . .

Trey had his head down, practically tucked between his knees. But the suspense was too much to bear. Trey, the biggest coward in the world, decided it was better to know what was about to happen. Silently, slowly, he tilted his head back.

A uniformed man—no, really just a boy, barely older than Trey himself—stood there silently looking down at him. Trey's eyes suddenly seemed to work like a camera, registering every detail of the boy's face in a single glance. The boy had freckles across his nose, and that detail alone seemed so out of place that Trey could do nothing but stare.

"*Liber?*" the boy said, oddly.

Wait a minute. Was he actually speaking *Latin?*

"Free?" Trey translated incredulously.

The boy rewarded him with such a small nod that Trey wondered if he'd imagined it. Because then the boy raised his walkie-talkie to his mouth and pressed the button on the side.

That's it, Trey thought, disappointment swelling through him. *Why didn't I fight when I had the chance? Why didn't I run?*

He probably still had a few seconds before the boy summoned the other uniformed men and they came swarming around the porch. But Trey couldn't move. He could just imagine where running or fighting would lead. He could hear the gunfire that was bound to come, could see the hands that would undoubtedly grab him, maybe pummel him—maybe beat him to death. . . .

It's better to be captured alive. To be meek and abiding. Then maybe they won't kill me right away.

No, they'd just torture him to try to get him to betray everyone he knew. No matter what, Trey couldn't win.

Then he heard what the boy shouted into his walkie-talkie.

"Porch all clear," he said. "Nothing here."

Trey stared up at the boy in amazement. He was so stunned, he couldn't make out the words that crackled out from the walkie-talkie in response.

"Affirmative," the boy said. "I'll join the search in the backyard right away."

He paused only long enough to glance at Trey one more time, and whisper, "Stay hidden." Then he turned on his heel and left.

Gradually, Trey's heart rate returned to normal—or at least what had passed for normal since he'd stepped out of the car, instead of the I'm-about-to-die rate his heart had reached when the boy was on the porch. He almost wondered if he'd been hallucinating. Could he have gone so insane with fear that he'd imagined the whole exchange?

Trey didn't think he had such a strong imagination.

He could hear bits and pieces of the continuing search—someone shouting for a shovel, another man grunting as he carried a heavy trunk to a car. But no one else stepped up onto the porch. Nobody else came to look for Trey. And Trey was so paralyzed with fear that he couldn't have disobeyed the boy's order if he'd wanted to.

Then, amazingly, he began to hear doors slamming, engines starting, cars driving away. They went slower now, their engines making the same letdown hum as fire trucks driving away after a fire. Trey tried to eavesdrop— he listened so hard that his ears roared. But he couldn't tell whether the men had found whatever they were looking for or not. They were talking about women; they were talking about smoking the cigars they'd discovered in Mr. Talbot's closet.

"Illegal as all get-out," one man said loudly.

"Yeah, we're just going to have to smoke them and destroy the evidence," another shouted back. "It's the least we can do for an old friend."

This made the men laugh, like it was funny that any of them might be friends with Mr. Talbot. Or maybe it was that Mr. Talbot had thought they were friends, but they weren't.

Trey could never understand what people meant when their words and meanings didn't match up.

That's called irony, he reminded himself. *I don't get irony. I admit it. Okay, Dad? Are you happy now?*

He was so busy carrying on an imaginary conversation with his father that he missed the exact moment when the last car drove away. For hours, it seemed, there had been a general hubbub all across the Talbots' property—raucous laughter, bossy shouts. But suddenly the entire area was plunged into an eerie silence. Trey strained his ears again, listening. He risked another peek over the top of the flowerpot. There were no more cars within sight or earshot. But he didn't have to wonder if he'd hallucinated everything, because the uniformed men had left behind plenty of evidence of their visit: trampled flowers, skid marks on the driveway, holes scattered in a seemingly random pattern across the yard.

Trey ducked out of sight again.

Maybe the chauffeur will bring Nina and the others back now, he thought. *Maybe the chauffeur knew somehow that the uniformed men were coming. And he'll know that they're gone now and it's safe to come back and get me.*

Trey didn't want to think about how the chauffeur might have known about the uniformed men. He didn't want to think about what that probably meant about whose side the chauffeur was on. He just wanted to be rescued.

Because if he wasn't rescued, he didn't have the slightest idea what he was supposed to do.

CHAPTER *THREE*

t got dark.

Trey's mind recoiled from calculating just how long that meant he'd been hiding behind the flowerpot. It had been early morning when he'd arrived at Mr. Talbot's house. It was dusk now. He'd waited a very long time.

Trey imagined what would happen if he never moved, if nobody ever came for him.

I'd die of hunger or thirst, he thought. *How long would it be before someone discovered my corpse?* Maybe he'd be a skeleton by then. *Nobody would know who I was.*

Trey was scaring himself. But he had to. He had to make it seem scarier to stay hidden than to venture out.

You're hungry now, aren't you? he challenged himself. *Aren't you starving? You've got to get some food.*

But his stomach, which had become more than accustomed to hunger over the years, just said, *Hey, don't pin this on me. I can wait.*

Trey's legs were stiff from huddling in one position for

MARGARET PETERSON HADDIX

so long. He thought maybe he'd been asleep part of the time, but it was a strange sort of sleep, where any noise, any hint of movement—a bird fluttering in the sky, say—could snap him to full alertness. Still, he'd managed to dream. He'd had strange dreams where his father was alive again, and standing on the porch lecturing him. Only, in the dream, Trey's ears didn't seem to be working, and he couldn't understand anything his father said. He could just tell that his father was very worried.

"Symbolism," Trey muttered to himself. "Dreams are often metaphorical representations of the dreamer's fears."

Or wishes.

Trey gave a little half-snort of disgust at himself, that he could think about symbolism and metaphors at a time like this. He needed to think about *action.* He needed a plan. He shook his head as if that would clear his mind of fancy, useless words and lingering dreams and cobwebs.

If the chauffeur and Nina and the others comes back . . .

They hadn't so far. Odds were, they weren't going to. Ever.

If Mr. Talbot comes back . . .

After being whisked off in handcuffs? Trey couldn't quite get his mind around what might have happened to Mr. Talbot—had those men in uniform been arresting him or kidnapping him? But Trey knew he couldn't hold out hope anymore that Mr. Talbot would be his salvation.

If Lee shows up . . .

Ah. There was a hope worth dwelling on. Lee had said

he'd meet his friends at Mr. Talbot's house. He hadn't said when, but he *would* come, and when he did, Trey didn't want to have to admit that he'd spent the whole time cowering on the porch.

So it was shame, finally, that made Trey stand up and shake out his stiff legs. He stepped off the side of the porch, so he could crouch behind a line of bushes next to the house. Between the darkness and the bushes, Trey could convince himself he was still hiding. That gave him the courage to keep walking, following the slope of the yard downhill. The bushes sheltered him so well that he kept going, even around a dark corner.

Then he saw a huge garage, gaping open. A dim light illuminated two gigantic luxury cars and a vacant space where a third belonged. Where a third had evidently been, until it had whisked Mr. Talbot away that morning.

Trey stared. He felt a silly little burst of pride, that he knew enough to label this space a garage. He'd never seen one before, except in pictures. And pictures, Trey had learned in his short time outside of hiding, never did anything justice. Everything was bigger in real life. Scarier.

Irreparably damaged. The words forced their way to Trey's attention as though they'd been waiting for him in the garage. They were from an argument his parents had had shortly before his father died.

"The boy's irreparably damaged now," his mother had screamed at his father. "Handicapped for life. He's got no chance of ever living a normal life. Of ever thinking a normal thought. Are you happy now? Is this what you wanted?"

Trey shut down his memory right then, wishing he'd never heard that fight, wishing his mind hadn't recorded it so well. His feet moved automatically across the garage floor, toward the door that hung open, leading to the house. His mind seemed incapable of thinking anything now beyond, *Hide inside. Better hiding always inside.*

The space he entered was dark, and that was just fine with Trey. With the door from the garage still open, he had just enough light to make out a long hallway, lined with doors. The doors were all shut, or else Trey wouldn't have had the courage to walk past them. As it was, he tip-toed.

Either Mr. Talbot and his family were all awful slobs or else the uniformed men had totally trashed the place. The hallway was littered with clothing and pillows and other items Trey couldn't identify without more light. He tried to step over them, but it was hard to find bare carpet to walk on. The items that were hardest to dodge were round and black and metal. They had holes in the middle—were they wheels of some sort? Why had the Talbots needed so many of them? Trey stubbed his toe on one, and it was all he could do not to cry out in pain. But he managed without a whimper.

Hey, silent pain is my specialty, he thought darkly, almost amusing himself.

And then he accidentally stepped squarely on one of

the disks, and it rocked against another one, making a dull thud. Trey froze, waiting. Surely the sound had been too soft to attract anyone's attention. Surely there was no one around to hear. Surely—

A line of light appeared near the ceiling, like a door opening. How could there be a door so high up? And then a figure appeared in the doorway, and a beam of light began sweeping down, down, down . . .

Right toward Trey.

Trey hit the floor, thinking he needed to dive under some of the clothing and pillows. But he only succeeded in hitting more of the metal wheels, hurting himself and making even more noise.

The light found him.

And up at the top of the room, behind the light, a woman began screaming.

CHAPTER *FOUR*

The screaming stopped as abruptly as it had begun.

"That's it. I'm done with my hysterical-woman act," a woman's voice said. "I'm calm and cool and collected now, and I'm holding all the advantages. I'll have you know this flash-light doubles as a gun, and I'm a good aim. So think very carefully before you try anything. Are you one of them?"

"One of who?" Trey asked. "I mean, one of whom?"

"If you have to ask, you probably aren't," the woman mused. "Good grief. The looters are arriving already."

The flashlight's beam was blinding him. Trey thought of a bullet following the same path.

"I'm not a looter!" he said urgently. "I'm—I'm—I'm a friend of Mr. Talbot's!"

The woman actually laughed.

"Right. You expect me to believe George has friends his wife has never met?"

Wife. So this was Mrs. Talbot?

Trey dared to relax a little. If this woman was married

to Mr. Talbot, she wouldn't turn him in to the Population Police. But how could he convince her to trust him?

She shone the light away from his face momentarily—checking, Trey realized, to make sure that he wasn't holding a weapon. He held up his hands slowly, in what he hoped would look like the international sign of surrender and goodwill.

"So, *friend,* what are you doing here?" Mrs. Talbot asked, returning the flashlight beam to his face. "Why did you show up today, of all days? And why didn't you just ring the doorbell, instead of sneaking in through our basement?"

"Oh, I did!" Trey said frantically. "But then I saw Mr. Talbot being taken away, and I was scared, and I didn't think anyone was here, and, see I was coming from the Grants' house—" Trey was just babbling now. All his skill with words seemed to have abandoned him.

"The Grants?" Mrs. Talbot interrupted. Something in her voice caught a little. "Oh, thank goodness! Why didn't you tell me right away? I was so scared. . . . I should have known the Grants would find out what happened and send someone to help me. What a relief!"

"Uh, ma'am?" Trey said. "The Grants are—" He stopped. Even he could tell that this probably wasn't a good time to inform her that Mr. and Mrs. Grant were dead, that it was their murders he had witnessed the night before, their deaths that had sent him running to Mr. Talbot for help. She seemed to think he was going to help her.

What if everyone is just looking for someone else to

save them? he wondered. It was a strange thought, and didn't seem to fit in his mind. It didn't match up with anything else he knew.

But Trey didn't have time to analyze it, because suddenly Mrs. Talbot switched off the flashlight and switched on a giant overhead light.

"All this darkness is giving me the creeps," Mrs. Talbot said. "And who needs it, if you're from the Grants?"

In the light, Trey could see everything. The disks that he'd knocked together were weights, meant to be attached to barbells. Rows of weight-lifting apparatus lined the far wall, but they'd all been torn apart. Pulleys hung oddly, benches were ripped from the frames—the room looked like a cyclone had hit it. Trey looked away, up a long staircase. Mrs. Talbot was standing at the top.

And Mrs. Talbot was . . . beautiful.

Trey had seen very few women in his life. If he didn't count girls, he'd actually known only one: his mother, who'd had frown lines etched around her mouth, worry lines carved into her brow, disappointment mirrored in her eyes. Trey's mother had worn shapeless dresses and mismatched, holey sweaters, one on top of the other, in a constant battle to stay warm. It seemed like she'd always had gray, lifeless hair; Trey had even wondered if she'd once been a gray-haired little girl.

Mrs. Talbot's hair was red—so bright and vibrant Trey was almost surprised he hadn't been able to see it in the dark. Her face was smooth and unlined. Even the fright of finding an intruder in her basement had apparently only given her skin a healthy-looking glow. And her body had curves. . . . Wasn't she somebody's mother? Mothers weren't supposed to look like that, were they?

Trey blushed, but couldn't stop staring.

"So what do the Grants want me to do?" Mrs. Talbot was saying. "I can be ready to leave in five minutes. I already have the car packed. How soon do they think they can get George out?"

"Ma'am?" Trey said, then blushed all the harder because "ma'am" seemed much too matronly a term for this woman. "They didn't—I mean—I can't—"

Mrs. Talbot's hand seemed to tighten on the flashlight.

"Did the Grants send you to help me or not?" she said sharply.

"I want to help you," Trey said. "Honest. I'll do my best. But—I don't know what I'm supposed to do."

Trey felt the weight of his words settling on his shoulders. It was like he'd lifted one of the barbells lying by his feet. He'd just promised to help Mrs. Talbot—what would that mean? And if he was going to take responsibility for her, where was it supposed to end? Was he also responsible for helping Mr. Talbot? For Nina and Joel and John? For Lee and Smits?

It was so much easier to think only of his own needs, his own life. But how could he not help?

"Oh," Mrs. Talbot said, and seemed to sag against the doorframe. For the first time, Trey realized that she was terrified, that she'd probably been even more panicked by the uniformed men than Trey was. This was her home, after all. It was her husband who'd been taken away in handcuffs. "Didn't the Grants give you any instructions at all?" she asked forlornly.

"The Grants are dead," Trey said brusquely. It seemed like he'd be lying if he didn't tell her now. "They were killed last night, at a party, by a man named Oscar. I was there. I saw it all."

Trey's memory flashed the whole strange scene at him once again: women in glittering ball gowns, men in tuxedos hiding guns, champagne in fluted glasses, and a huge chandelier cut loose and plunging down. . . .

"Dead?" Mrs. Talbot repeated. "Dead?" Her eyes flooded with tears, and she sank down to the top step of the stairs. "Oh, my friends," she murmured.

"They owed you money," Trey said. Amazingly, he was still holding the stack of papers he'd taken from Mr. Grant's desk. He waved the whole sheaf of papers at Mrs. Talbot now, as though that would remind her that the Grants had not been just friends. "They owed you and Mr. Talbot two hundred and fifty thousand dollars."

Mrs. Talbot shrugged, like money didn't matter.

"So many deaths," she muttered, and Trey remembered that the Talbots' daughter Jen—another illegal child—had died too. What if Mrs. Talbot started sobbing now, or wailing, or going into total hysterics? Trey really wouldn't know what to do then. But Mrs. Talbot only sniffed once, in a dignified way. Then she began speaking quietly, look-ing not at Trey, but at the blank wall opposite her.

"George said there was danger," she said. "We sent the boys away to boarding school in September. Just in case."

Boys? Then Trey realized that for Jen to be an illegal third child, she'd had to have had siblings. They must have been brothers.

"And George and I, we had drills. What if they come for him in the middle of the night? What if they come for him during breakfast? What if, what if, what if? I did every-thing right. Just like I was supposed to. I hid in our secret room. For hours. You know what I did in there? I was painting my toenails." Mrs. Talbot looked down at Trey and grinned, ever so slightly. "My little way of saying, hey, you can't scare me. But after—after I came out, the plan was always for me to go to the Grants' house for help. If I hadn't checked the TV, I'd be at the Grants' by now. And what would I have found there?"

Trey tried not to think about the scene of destruction he'd left.

"What did you see on TV?" he asked. "That stopped you from leaving?"

"Huh?" Mrs. Talbot said. "Oh. Riots. They said there was rioting in the streets, so I thought, might as well wait until morning to leave."

Riots? Trey and his friends had seen nothing like that on their trip from the Grants' house to the Talbots', but it had been the middle of the night. The riots must have started during the day, after Mr. Talbot was arrested, while Mrs. Talbot and Trey were hiding. *Riots,* Trey thought. A strange emotion began growing inside him. Hope.

Maybe this is it. It's beginning. Maybe riots were what the resistance leaders had planned, to get the Government to change the Population Law. Maybe third children aren't even illegal anymore. Maybe the riots have already worked.

Trey's friend Lee had been determined, for as long as Trey had known him, to change the Government, so third children could be free from hiding, free from using fake identities if they ever wanted to go out. Before Lee, Trey had had another friend, Jason, who had said he'd wanted the same thing. But Jason had been lying, and that had been enough to make Trey wonder if he could ever trust anyone.

But maybe now, maybe with the riots . . . Trey remembered another fact that gave him even more hope: Mr. Talbot was a double agent. Publicly, he said he opposed third children. He worked for the Population Police, a group that had been created solely to catch third children and the people who hid them. But secretly, under cover, Mr. Talbot sabotaged his employer, rescuing illegal children and giving them fake I.D.'s. Maybe if the Population Law had been eliminated, the Government had decided to arrest everyone who worked for the Population Police. So of course Mr. Talbot would have been arrested too. Maybe Trey and Lee and their other friends would just have to testify about Mr. Talbot's true beliefs, and they'd be able to rescue him. Maybe Trey could help Mrs. Talbot after all.

Then Trey remembered something else.

"They told about the riots on TV?" he said incredulously. "That's impossible. They'd never tell about something like that."

Trey himself had never seen a television. But he'd heard his father say that it only broadcast propaganda. "Think they'd ever let a TV anchor say anything bad about the Government?" Trey's father had taunted his mother once. "Think they'd ever say anything that didn't make it seem like our country is paradise itself?"

Riots didn't belong in paradise.

Mrs. Talbot snorted.

"Well, not on regular TV, of course," she said. "The Baron channels."

"What?" Trey said. He'd always known that the Government allowed some people to have special privileges. The Barons, as they were called, were rich while everyone else was poor. They had so much food they could afford to throw it away—while everyone else scrambled to get dry crusts or pretended that moldy cheese was perfectly fine. They lived in fine mansions, while everyone else crowded together, entire families in a single room.

Trey hadn't known that the Barons even had their own TV channels.

"You can't expect us to trust the regular broadcasts," Mrs. Talbot said defensively. "We Barons need . . . information that other people don't."

"But how do they do that?" Trey asked. He tried to

remember how television signals were transmitted. "How can the signals go to some TVs and not to others?"

"Some sort of special cable, I guess," Mrs. Talbot said with a shrug. "Come on. I'll show you."

She seemed relieved to be talking about something ordinary, like TV, instead of death and danger and foiled plans. Trey stood up and began climbing the stairs.

Surreal, he thought. *This entire day has been so surreal I don't even know what to be afraid of anymore.*

He followed Mrs. Talbot out the basement door and down a long hallway. They reached a huge room full of wide couches and coffee tables. It had probably been an extraordinarily beautiful room originally, but, like the basement, it was a mess now. Only the enormous screen covering a large portion of one wall seemed intact. Mrs. Talbot stepped over ripped cushions and picked up a black remote control from one of the coffee tables. She hit a button on the remote, and the screen seemed to come to life, with gray and black and white dots dancing across the surface. It was a fascinating sight, like some of the bizarre artwork Trey had seen in books.

"See?" Mrs. Talbot said. "The regular stations are off the air. So what else is new." She flipped through the channels, bringing up momentary darkness, then more patterns of random dots. "Now here's the first Baron channel."

She hit another button, and the screen filled up with a serious-looking man.

". . . continues in virtually all parts of the city," he was saying. "Our advice to you would be to remain at home until further notice. In other news—"

Suddenly the man's voice broke off and his face disappeared, replaced by more of the dots. Trey glanced over at Mrs. Talbot, but she hadn't changed the channel. She was standing there looking as stunned as Trey felt.

"That's odd," Mrs. Talbot muttered. "They're usually so reliable."

She hit a few more buttons, zipping though channels. None of the stations appeared to be broadcasting. Then suddenly another man's face appeared, first wavering, with rolling black lines, then solidifying and filling the entire screen. Mrs. Talbot gasped, but Trey was staring so intently at the TV screen that he barely heard her.

"Good evening, fellow citizens," the man on TV said. He was wearing a luxurious black jacket, with gold trim on the collar and over the sleeves. "I am delighted to inform you that the old, corrupt Government of General Terus has fallen to the will of the people. General Terus was placed under arrest at seven thirty this evening. I assure you that my squads will restore peace throughout the land quite soon. I am fully in control and I pledge to all of you, my loyal citizens, that I will live up to the trust you have always placed in me. I—"

Trey missed the next few words, because Mrs. Talbot had begun frantically flipping through the channels again. The man in the gold-trimmed uniform was on every station.

"—peace and prosperity—"

"—work together—"

"—true to the cause I've always believed in—"

With the moments of silence between changing channels, Trey could hardly make sense of the man's message. It didn't matter. He'd heard enough. Enough to make him delirious with joy.

"It happened," he muttered. Then he screamed, "It happened! I'm free! All third children are free!"

Mrs. Talbot was looking at him strangely. Of course. She wouldn't have known that he was an illegal third child with a fake I.D. Trey didn't care. He wouldn't have to care ever again about who knew the truth.

"Young man," she said, almost sternly. "Don't you know who that is?" She pointed at the TV.

Trey stopped shouting long enough to glance at the televised man. He had white hair, a mustache, dark eyes, thin lips. And he didn't look the slightest bit familiar. Trey was pretty sure he'd never seen so much as a picture of him.

"No," Trey said. "But who cares? General Terus is gone."

"Oh, you should care, all right," Mrs. Talbot said. "That man"—and she pointed at the TV screen again, almost accusingly, and her voice shook—"that man is Aldous Krakenaur."

"Who?" Trey said.

"The head of the Population Police," Mrs. Talbot said.

And then she bent her head down and began to sob.

CHAPTER *FIVE*

T rey went numb.

Euphoria to horror in one second will do that to a guy, he thought, and was almost relieved that some part of his brain was still available to think.

He'd always thought he was a pessimist—he'd never fully believed in Lee's rosy dreams of freedom for all third children. But even Trey had never imagined news this bad.

"Are you sure?" he asked Mrs. Talbot.

She stopped sobbing just long enough to give him a withering look.

"Well, maybe . . ." Trey was searching for some reason to still hold on to some hope. "Maybe he won't be any worse than General Terus. I mean, General Terus wanted all third children dead. This guy—what's he going to do? Kill us twice?"

Mrs. Talbot wiped her eyes and glared at Trey.

"Aldous Krakenaur is insane. He hates third children beyond all reason," she said. "He was always complaining that General Terus didn't devote enough resources to hunting them down. And now—now there'll be house-to-house searches. Traffic stopped on every street. Identity records scoured for fakes, again and again. No third child will be able to survive."

Mrs. Talbot's words chilled Trey so thoroughly that he almost missed her whispering, at the end, "Maybe it's good that Jen is already dead."

On the TV screen, Aldous Krakenaur was smiling.

". . . And together, we will make our country great again," he said.

Mrs. Talbot threw the remote straight at the screen. The glass shattered and sparks flew. Then the screen was dark and dead, finally matching the rest of the destroyed room.

"Why did you do that?" Trey complained. "Now we won't know what's going on."

"I don't want to know," Mrs. Talbot said. "I know too much already."

She collapsed onto the nearest couch and stared vacantly at the broken TV. Trey remained standing, awkwardly. He wasn't exactly adept at interpersonal relationships under the best of circumstances. What in the world was he supposed to do now?

He closed his eyes briefly, and everything he'd witnessed that day seemed to replay in his memory. Mr. Talbot coming to the door, failing to recognize Trey. . . .

Or did he recognize me after all? Was he really just trying to warn me away—me and the rest of my "team"? The thought made Trey feel a little better, even though the warning hadn't helped. There hadn't been time to do anything before Mr. Talbot was whisked away . . .

A new thought occurred to Trey.

"Mrs. Talbot?" he said. "I don't blame you for being upset and all over Aldous Krakenaur. I mean, I'm glad you don't want him in control. But isn't this good for your husband? I mean, he works for the Population Police, and Aldous Krakenaur's in charge of the Population Police. . . . Mr. Talbot was taken away before the Government changed. Wouldn't Aldous Krakenaur set him free? Maybe this Krakenaur guy's already heard about what happened to Mr. Talbot and already sent him home. Maybe Mr. Talbot's on his way here, right now."

Slowly Mrs. Talbot turned her head to stare up at Trey.

"Aldous always hated George," she said. "The only thing that kept George in power at the Population Police headquarters was his friendship with General Terus."

"Mr. Talbot was friends with the president?" Trey's voice actually squeaked, he was so amazed.

"He pretended to be friends," Mrs. Talbot said. "But now if General Terus is gone . . . They probably arrested George this morning so he wouldn't warn the president what was coming."

"Well, he can't warn him now—looks like the coup is over," Trey said. "So maybe they'll set Mr. Talbot free because there's no point in holding him any longer."

Mrs. Talbot went back to staring at the broken TV.

"You're just a little boy, aren't you?" she said in an eerily calm voice, as if nothing really mattered anymore. "All the thirds—so naïve. So sheltered. Don't you know? The only way they're going to release George is in a coffin."

Trey gulped.

"No they aren't," he said, arguing with more conviction than he felt. "You can rescue him. I'll—I'll help."

What was he saying? What if Mrs. Talbot took him up on his offer?

"I don't know where they're holding him," Mrs. Talbot said, still in the same dead voice.

"Then find out," Trey said. He wanted Mrs. Talbot to stop acting so strange. He wanted her to take control and fix everything. "Don't you have any friends in the Population Police?" he asked. "Anyone you can trust?"

At first, Trey thought Mrs. Talbot hadn't heard his question. Then she slowly answered, "I don't trust a single soul in this country right now. I don't even trust you. How do I know you weren't lying to me about the Grants?"

"Because I wasn't," Trey said frantically. "Because—why would I want to lie?"

"I don't know," Mrs. Talbot said. "I don't care." She stood up abruptly, seeming to shake off her stupor. "I'm leaving. Good-bye."

She brushed past him. Trey felt like he was being abandoned all over again.

It's just like when Mom left me. . . . He shut out the thought immediately.

"Wait!" he yelled after Mrs. Talbot. "Where are you going?"

"That's none of your business," she called back over her shoulder.

"Can I—can I go with you?" It was humiliating even to ask. But no more humiliating than being abandoned in silence.

"No," Mrs. Talbot said. She paused in front of the door that led to the basement and on out to the garage. "But I will give you some advice. Don't hang around here for long. When governments fall . . . Well, they won't leave this place empty. Spoils of war and all that." She looked around, as if noticing the mess for the first time. She reached out to a nearby shelf to touch a delicate crystal vase that had miraculously escaped destruction. Trey decided it must have some sentimental value. Maybe Mr. Talbot had given it to her years ago, and she couldn't bear to leave it behind.

Then Mrs. Talbot lifted the vase off the shelf and hurled it to the floor. It smashed instantly into dozens of tiny shards.

"There," Mrs. Talbot said grimly. "They're welcome to it. They're welcome to it all."

She walked out the door and was gone.

CHAPTER SIX

Trey hid.

It wasn't something he thought about. One minute he was standing by the door that Mrs. Talbot had just shut in his face, the next he was cowering in a kitchen cupboard. All the pots and pans from the cabinet had been thrown out on the floor; that's why he'd noticed it. Otherwise he might have hidden in a closet or under a sofa or behind a bookcase. . . .

There wasn't much room in the cupboard, and he'd begun shivering so hard—no, it was really shaking, shaking with fear—that he kept banging his elbows and knees against the hard wood around him. He could have moved to another hiding space, but that would have required more courage and will than he had after being abandoned and left in danger yet again.

But she was so beautiful . . . , he thought vaguely, and then was irritated with himself. Why was it any different to be abandoned by a beautiful woman than by an ugly one?

No, he corrected himself. *Mom wasn't ugly. She was just . . . defeated.*

He had never thought of it that way before. Mom had lost Dad too, after all. She'd lost her husband, she'd lost all hope—what was there left for her to live for?

Me, Trey thought fiercely, and it was like he was answering a question about himself, not his mother. It made him stop shaking, momentarily. It made him think that he might be feeling light-headed because of hunger, not just horror.

I am in a kitchen, he reminded himself. *There's probably food mere inches away. All I have to do is open the door of this cupboard.* How stupid and cowardly was he to sit there shaking and starving instead of eating?

Trey pushed the door of the cupboard open a crack. In the dim light that filtered in from the TV room, he could see a refrigerator. He shoved out one foot and then the other, carefully avoiding all the pots and pans on the floor. He angled the rest of his body out of the cupboard. Crouching, he reached over and opened the refrigerator.

The sudden bright light scared him, but he reached in and blindly grabbed garishly colored cartons and containers. Then, clutching the food, he dove back into the cupboard.

There wasn't room in the cupboard to eat with the door shut, so he risked leaving it open. That way, he could even see what he was eating. A paper carton yielded rice and

mysterious vegetables in a spicy sauce, all of which he virtually inhaled. He'd also grabbed three plastic containers
of strawberry yogurt. This was harder to eat with his fingers, so he mainly squeezed it into his mouth and then
licked out the containers as best he could.

Like an animal, he thought. *I'm behaving like an animal.*

He remembered his father's view of animals. One night,
years ago, Dad had told Trey and his mother about seeing
feral cats in an alley on his way home from work. Trey was
pretty young then, but he already knew Latin.

"Feral?" Trey had said. "Like *fera,* meaning 'beast,' or *fer-
alis,* 'funeral'? Were the cats dead?"

Dad had ruffled Trey's hair fondly. Trey's knowledge of
Latin always made Dad fond.

"Very good, son!" he'd said. "The word can be used in
either sense. But in this case, it means 'wild beast.' Those
cats used to be somebody's pets, but now they're out living on their own."

Trey was intrigued. He'd followed Dad around the rest
of the evening, asking questions.

"How can those cats live on their own?" he asked as Dad
took off his good coat—the one with only one patch on
the sleeve. "Who feeds them? Who gives them books to
read?" In Trey's world then, books were as important as
food. And books were more plentiful.

"Animals don't read books," Dad said. "They aren't like
humans. Animals are only concerned with surviving—
with eating and . . . and reproducing. That's what separates

humans from animals—our ability to think and reason. To do more than just survive."

And then Dad had exchanged a significant glance with Mom. That's what had made the whole conversation stick in Trey's mind. Trey hadn't understood that glance.

But now, remembering, he was ashamed. How ashamed Dad would be if he could see Trey now, not thinking, not reasoning, just trying to survive.

But Dad, you never did tell me who took care of those cats, he thought resentfully.

Trey squashed the three yogurt containers and put them in the paper carton that had held the rice and vegetables. Bravely, he inched his way over to a trash can and threw away the garbage. Then he scurried back to his cupboard and pulled the door shut behind him.

Okay, I'm thinking now. What am I going to do?

He felt drawn in so many different directions.

"Stay hidden," the boy in uniform had said on the porch. Why? Why hadn't the boy reported him? Could Trey trust his advice?

"I'll do my best to help you," Trey had promised Mrs. Talbot. Was that promise void now because she'd left?

"I'll tell Mr. Talbot everything," Trey had promised Lee. But now Trey couldn't even remember where he'd left the papers from Mr. Grant's desk, the ones he'd wanted to show to Mr. Talbot.

"I'll watch out for Lee," Trey had promised Mr. Hendricks before leaving for the Grants' party yesterday—

had that been only yesterday? It felt like a century ago.

Mr. Hendricks. Of course. Why hadn't Trey thought of him sooner?

Mr. Hendricks was the headmaster of Trey's school. He'd been in a horrible accident as a young man and lost the lower portions of his legs. So he used a wheelchair to get around. Last night, when Trey and his friends had witnessed a murder and were terrified of the muscular killer, they hadn't even thought of going to a disabled man for help.

I'm sorry, Trey thought, as if Mr. Hendricks could overhear his thoughts. *You're so much more reliable than Mr. Talbot. Smarter, too.*

All Trey needed was a phone. He'd have to be careful what he said—the Population Police tapped the phone lines—but he could speak in code. And then Mr. Hendricks would have someone come and pick him up, and Lee too when he arrived. It was that easy.

For a moment Trey thought about waiting in his cupboard until Lee came—let Lee make the phone call. Let Lee figure out how to make "Come get us immediately!" sound innocuous and dull to phone-tapping listeners. Let Lee take care of everything.

But as familiar shame washed over him, Trey thought, *No. I have to do this.* Mrs. Talbot had warned that someone from the new Government might be taking over the Talbots' house. What if Trey dallied and waited for Lee, and then the Government captured both boys—because of Trey?

I can do this, Trey told himself. He'd never actually used a telephone, but he understood the process. He could call information, ask for Hendricks School. . . . The only hard part was getting the courage to leave his cupboard.

Maybe there's a phone in the kitchen, Trey told himself. *Maybe I won't have to go very far at all.*

That thought got him out of the cupboard. He picked his way past the pots and pans yet again and crawled along the floor. His cupboard—he was thinking longingly of it as "his" now—was under a counter smack in the middle of the kitchen. He circled this island, staring up at every counter and wall. Sometimes phones hung on walls, didn't they?

It was hard to tell, because the counters were covered with a blizzard of papers, hiding the walls from view. A closet hung open, with an avalanche of boxed food thrown out on the floor. Trey resisted the urge to stop and scoop some spilled cereal into his mouth.

See, Dad? he thought. *I'm not an animal.*

He worked up the courage to step into the TV room, where the lights were still on.

The curtains are drawn, he reminded himself. *You're still safe. No one can see you.*

He circled the room, stepping over broken glass, ripped-up pillows.

He found the phone on the floor, under a couch. He pulled it out easily—the hard plastic receiver, the curly cord, the—

Nothing else came out from under the couch. The curly cord had been cut.

Against all logic, Trey held the receiver up to his ear anyway. He listened to the sound of dead air, of no connection whatsoever to the outside world.

Desperation made Trey brave. He searched the entire house. He found four more phones and a computer modem.

All with severed cords.

Holding the last phone in an upstairs bedroom, Trey began whimpering, exactly like a wounded animal.

Lee, it's all up to you now, he thought. *Come quickly. Oh, please, come soon.*

CHAPTER *SEVEN*

ee didn't show up. Days passed, and Trey waited
patiently, but he heard no doorbell, no knock at the
door, no cheerful voice calling out, "Hey! Where is everyone?"

Dimly, Trey knew he should be grateful that nobody
else showed up either—no more men in uniform, no family newly authorized to steal the Talbots' house. But it was
so hard to wait, always wondering what had happened to
his friends, to Mr. and Mrs. Talbot, to the entire country.

*The head of the Population Police is in charge of the
Government now,* he reminded himself. *What do you
think's happening? Peace and joy and happiness?*

Most of the time, Trey felt the same near-panic he'd
experienced barely a year earlier, waiting for his mother to
return from his father's funeral. He'd been too grief-
stricken and bewildered then even to read, and he kept
trying to imagine his life without Dad.

Will Mom take over teaching me Latin and French and

Greek? he'd wondered. *Will she talk to me in the evenings instead of glaring resentfully while I study?* In between his bouts of anguish, Trey had felt almost hopeful, imagining Mom finally taking care of him—loving him—like mothers did in books.

It'd been beyond his imagination to think that she would get rid of him.

Now, wandering aimlessly through the Talbots' huge house, Trey kept wondering about Lee.

Has he forgotten his friends? Has he forgotten how badly he wants to make third children free? Or is he too scared of the new Government to show his face in public again?

It was this last question that worried Trey the most. If even Lee was scared, then Trey should be terrified, petrified, frightened out of his wits.

Sometimes he was.

On the third day, the electricity in the Talbots' house went off. It happened at dusk, just as the lights that Trey had left on—one in the TV room, one in the basement— had begun to seem cozy and threatening all at once. In a split second Trey lost the lights, the refrigerator's hum, the heating system's purr.

Cautiously, he stepped over to a window and peeked out. The whole neighborhood had gone dark—every huge house on the Talbots' street had been plunged into blackness.

Every single one of them looked dead.

Trey moved to the back of the house, to a window in the TV room. Only one small house stood behind the Talbots'. It was dark too, but as Trey watched, he saw dim, flicker-ing lights—candles?—spring to life inside, throwing shadows around tiny rooms.

A woman stood at the back door of the small house, and a boy came up beside her. He said something to her, and she nodded. Then the boy scampered out the door, across the yard, and into another building—a barn?—off to the side.

Trey blinked. Maybe his eyes were playing tricks on him. Maybe the uncertain light had fooled him.

Or maybe the boy was someone Trey knew. Not Lee— Trey would have instantly run out of the house, screaming with joy, if he'd thought it was Lee. No, he thought the boy he'd seen was Smits Grant, the boy Lee had taken to safety.

And wherever Smits was, Lee had to be too.

Didn't he?

CHAPTER *EIGHT*

Trey began thinking very strategically.

First, he ate as much of the food from the stopped refrigerator and freezer as he could, before it spoiled. He drank nearly a gallon of milk, gobbled down a frozen dinner, forced himself to swallow a pint of ice cream—a delicacy he'd never had before, but that seemed cloyingly sweet after the first two bites. He ate it anyway.

Then he set up a lookout station beside the TV room window. If the boy wasn't Smits, Trey didn't want to reveal himself. But if Smits and Lee had been staying in the house behind the Talbots' the whole time . . . well, Trey wanted to get over there as soon as possible.

The boy stayed in the barn for a very long time.

When he came out, it was too dark for Trey to see anything but a shadowy shape. Disappointment bit at the back of Trey's throat, but he forced himself to sit still and wait and watch some more.

The boy went into the house, where the candles were

still glowing in the windows. Maybe with the candlelight, Trey would be able to see—

Somebody drew the drapes.

Trey was so frustrated that he kicked over one of the few coffee tables that the uniformed men had left upright.

But after a little while, the boy came outside again— Trey was sure it was the same boy. He stood in the doorway of the house and seemed to be saying something over his shoulder, to someone Trey couldn't see.

Trey dared to open the TV room window, just a crack. If he couldn't see, maybe at least he'd be able to hear something. If only it was Lee's voice . . .

Faintly, Trey heard someone call out, ". . . too late in the year for fireflies."

And the boy in the doorway called back, "No it isn't. I see one. There!" And he pointed at a tiny gleam of light hovering near a bush by the barn.

Trey couldn't tell if the voices were Smits's and Lee's; they were too far away. And besides, Trey's ears weren't working too well—every sound he heard right now was distorted by his hopes and fears.

He'd have to go out there and see for himself if the boy was really Smits.

Daringly, Trey reached over to a full-length glass door beside his spying window. With trembling hands, he unlocked it and slid it open. Then he took a deep breath and stepped outside.

The night air felt cool and menacing on his face. Trey

grimaced and reminded himself that he had the cover of darkness to protect him, that he was in no greater danger outdoors than he'd been while cowering inside the Talbots' house.

You're probably even safer now, he told himself. *You could have been trapped indoors if someone dangerous showed up.*

Trey could think that—but he couldn't quite believe it. Outdoors was always scarier than indoors, no matter what.

Inching forward, Trey kept his gaze fixed on the boy. He was running around his backyard now, chasing a tiny pin-point of light that flashed off and on. Trey reached a line of trees that separated the Talbots' yard from the boy's. Trey squinted, trying frantically to tell if the boy was Smits, but against the lights of the house, the boy was just a dark silhouette.

Wrong angle, Trey thought. *As long as the boy's between me and the light, I'm never going to be able to see him clearly. Same principle as a solar eclipse.*

Pleased that his knowledge had been useful for once, Trey crept toward the barn and crawled behind a bush. Now he was closer to the light, but there wasn't enough of it to illuminate the boy's face, no matter where the boy was in the yard. Suddenly the boy dashed right past Trey's hiding place, and, without thinking, Trey reached out and grabbed him.

The boy screamed. Trey slapped his hand over the boy's

mouth, whirled him around, and held him against the side of the barn.

"Smits!" he hissed into the boy's ear. "Are you Smits Grant?"

The boy began to shake his head violently. Trey moved his hand back a little.

"No! I'm—I'm Peter Goodard! I'm—help!"

Trey clapped his hand over the boy's mouth again. No matter how much he denied it, the boy was Smits; Trey had finally recognized the voice. Now Trey just had to get Smits to recognize him.

"Smits! It's okay. It's me—Trey. I'm just looking for Lee—"

Out of nowhere, a fist walloped the side of Trey's face. He lost his balance and crashed through the branches of the bush, plunging straight to the ground and pulling Smits along with him.

"Hey, Peter," a deeper voice said from above them. "This punk bothering you?"

Trey looked up at the dark figure looming over him. Somehow, not being able to see the boy's—the man's?—face made him even scarier.

"Anybody messes with Peter, you've got to answer to me," the voice continued.

Trey huddled in terror on the ground.

"No, no, you don't understand," Trey pleaded. "I know Smits. Or Peter—whatever he's calling himself now. I just want him to tell me where one of my friends is. Smits, come on, you've got to remember me. . . ."

Trey could see that the person standing over him was rearing his fist back, ready to punch Trey again. Trey flinched, waiting for the inevitable pain, and Smits tried to squirm away. Trey managed to keep his hand over Smits's mouth until the last minute when he let go just so he could protect his own face with both hands.

Then Smits called out, "Wait, Mark! Don't hit him! This really is a friend of Lee's. And a friend of mine."

Trey dared to peek out between his fingers. The hulking figure above him—Mark?—had relaxed his fists.

"A friend? Why didn't you say so sooner?" Mark growled.

"Trey had his hand over my mouth and I couldn't talk," Smits said matter-of-factly.

Great, Trey thought. *I almost caused my own death by muzzling Smits.* He felt totally drained suddenly. *Aftereffects of an adrenaline surge,* he told himself.

"Look," he mustered the energy to say, "Lee can straighten all this out. Just get Lee to come out here and explain."

Smits sat up. It seemed like the moon had risen just in the past few minutes, and now its beams fell directly on Smits's face. Even in such dim light, Trey could tell that Smits looked baffled.

"But, Trey," Smits said, "I thought Lee was with you. The chauffeur came and got him that very first day."

CHAPTER *NINE*

Trey felt like Mark really had punched him again. He reeled back against the hard ground, then began to moan.

"Nooooo . . ."

"What's wrong with him?" Mark asked.

"I don't know," Smits said. "Trey, stop it! You're scaring me."

Trey didn't care. Why shouldn't everyone be as frightened as he was?

Mark slapped him, and Trey was stunned into silence.

"Hey!" Mark said. "That really *does* work on hysterical people. Always wanted to try that."

He sounded so cheerful, Trey wanted to hit him back.

"Everything all right out there?" a man called from the little house.

"Sure, Dad," Mark hollered back. "We're just fooling around. We'll go into the barn now so we won't bother you."

He hustled Smits and Trey toward a door. Trey wondered if he should object—was this Mark guy dangerous?—but he didn't have the will for resistance.

"Mother and Dad are so freaked out right now, 'cause of the news," Mark was saying. "And they don't like strangers nohow. So—why tell them you're here?"

Trey kept silent as they stepped into the barn and Mark shut the door behind them. It was so dark Trey could have walked into a wall with no warning whatsoever. He stayed as close to the door as possible.

"I know Dad's got an old lantern around here somewhere," Mark was muttering. "Oh, here it is."

He struck a match and a light flared, then settled into a dim glow. Now Trey could see pitchforks and hoes leaning against the wall. The lantern cast eerie shadows, making the pitchforks seem giant-size and terrifying. Trey had never been in a barn before, but this one seemed straight out of his worst nightmares.

"Okay," Mark said, as comfortably as if they were sitting down for tea in a cozy parlor. "Why'd you get so upset about L—uh, Lee, going off with that guy in the big fancy car?"

Now that they were indoors—even in a terrifying indoors—Trey realized that Mark was barely taller than Trey, and probably not much older. He wasn't some hulking muscle man, some horrifying monster—he was just another kid. He even had a little twang in his voice that reminded Trey of Lee.

Was Mark Lee's real brother?

"You can call him Luke around Trey," Smits said. "Trey knows that Luke was just pretending to be Lee. You're a third kid too, aren't you, Trey?"

Trey stiffened. How could Smits act so casual about everything? Lee was Trey's best friend, and even to him Trey had never actually come out and said, "I'm an illegal third child with a fake I.D. You are too, aren't you, Lee? I'll tell you my real name if you tell me yours." Trey *hadn't* known that Lee's real name was Luke. He and Lee just understood each other. They both understood that if you slipped and revealed a crumb of information about your real life—your real family, your real past, your real name—a true friend would just nod and go on.

"Whose question you gonna answer?" Mark asked. "Mine or the kid's?"

Trey looked from Mark to Smits and said, "I think Lee is in danger."

Smits screwed up his face like he was going to cry. Mark just leaned back against the wall, his posture clearly indicating, "Nothing you say's going to bother me."

"Why?" Mark challenged.

Quickly Trey explained what had happened when he'd arrived at the Talbots', how the chauffeur had abandoned him and kidnapped the other kids.

"He must have swung by here and picked up Lee right after that," Trey finished. "Why didn't anyone stop him?"

Even Mark looked worried now. He didn't answer.

"The chauffeur didn't kidnap Lee," Smits said in a small voice. "Lee *wanted* to go. The chauffeur drove by, and stopped and talked to Lee, and then Lee came inside and said he had to leave right away."

From Smits's forlorn expression, Trey guessed that for him, at least, Lee's leaving had been a little more compli- cated than that. Regardless of what I.D. card he might carry now, Smits was a real Grant, raised in unbelievable luxury. But Smits had been devastated by the deaths of first his brother, then his parents. Smits had clung to Lee as his substitute brother. Smits had probably cried when Lee left.

"It happened while I was at school," Mark said. "Luke said he'd still be here when I got home. So why'd he go off again so quick?"

There was pain in Mark's voice. He turned his face toward the shadows like he didn't want Trey or Smits to see the pain in his expression.

Maybe even this tough-guy Mark cried when Lee left, Trey thought. *Nobody ever cried over me.*

"Reckon that driver guy tricked Luke?" Mark said fiercely, like he was determined to turn all his pain into anger. "Tricked him into thinking he had to go, no matter what?"

"Yes," Trey whispered.

His whisper seemed to echo in the silent barn. The lantern flickered, making the shadows dance even more eerily along the walls.

"Luke went back to the Grants' house," Mark said, his voice as hard as rock, and about as likely to betray any emotion.

"He did?" Smits said. "I didn't know that."

Trey saw a full play of sorrow and fear in the younger boy's face.

"I heard Mother and Dad talking," Mark admitted. "They didn't know I was listening. Why . . ." He paused, steadying his voice. "Why do you reckon Luke would want to go back there?"

"I don't know," Trey said. "He wouldn't. We'd just come from there."

And we'd seen people die there. We didn't know if we could trust anyone there, Trey thought, but didn't say.

"The chauffeur was bad!" Smits said, his voice edging into hysteria. "What if he hurts Lee? What if he took him away to kill him?"

"Calm down," Trey said, trying to quell his own panic as much as Smits's. "We don't know anything about the chauffeur's intentions. If the chauffeur was going to hurt Lee or the others, he could have done it before he brought all of us here."

"You were in the car then," Smits said, pouting. "You were helping protect us."

Trey was so stunned by Smits's interpretation that he couldn't speak.

Protecting you? He wanted to say. *I was more terrified than anyone.* During the whole trip from the Grants' house to the Talbots', Trey had buried his nose in the Grants' financial records. All those numbers had seemed like Trey's only lifeline to sanity. Had Smits actually been fooled into thinking that Trey *wasn't* drowning in fear? That Trey might actually have been capable of taking care of someone else?

Had the chauffeur been fooled?

Mark narrowed his eyes and peered at Trey. Mark didn't look like he thought Trey would be much of a bodyguard.

"Seems like, if this driver was a good guy, if he had good reasons for taking my brother away, he wouldn't have left you behind," Mark said slowly.

Yes, Trey thought. *Exactly.* He liked Mark a little better for saying that.

"And the chauffeur went away before all the men in uniforms showed up," Trey said. "So he wasn't scared about his own safety. He left me behind on purpose." It hurt just to speak those words, but Trey forced them out. It was like he actually had some hope that Mark could help.

"So this dangerous man took Luke away and left you behind, and we don't know why," Mark said. He kicked the toe of his boot at the packed-dirt floor of the barn. "And did you hear that the Population Police are in control of everything now? Mother and Dad are inside listening to the radio right now, shaking in their shoes, scared to death. It's like the whole world's ending, but it hasn't quite ended yet way out here. And what they're most scared of is that something bad's going to happen to Luke, and they won't even know." He kicked the dirt once more, then looked up. "Let's go get him."

"Huh?" Trey said. He'd gotten lost in Mark's reasoning after that first kick in the dirt.

"You heard me," Mark said. "I said let's go get him. We'll go to the Grants' house and bring Luke back and every-thing will be okay."

Trey's jaw dropped in disbelief. He'd always thought Lee was insanely brave. Now he knew Lee's brother was even crazier.

"We don't have to go anywhere," Trey finally managed to say. "We can call. We can call the Grants' house, or call Mr. Hendricks back at the school—Mr. Hendricks can get Lee from the Grants' house, if we just call . . ."

He really meant that Mark could call. Mark or his par-ents. Trey was feeling better now, at the thought that somebody else could take care of everything and he wouldn't have to. This was a good plan.

But Mark was shaking his head.

"The Population Police shut down all the phone lines in the country yesterday—security reasons, they said. And now they've shut off the electricity. . . . What if they come and take away our gasoline next? We can't just sit around waiting. We've got to go rescue Luke."

He sounded almost happy at the thought that it would take more than a phone call to find his brother.

"We don't know for sure where he is," Trey protested.

He was suddenly desperate to avoid being roped into Mark's dangerous plan. "For all we know, the chauffeur might have lied about going back to the Grants' house. Trying to find Lee would be like . . . like looking for a needle in a haystack." He thought Mark might appreciate the agricultural analogy. But it didn't go far enough. He remembered what Mrs. Talbot had said about roadblocks and house-to-house searches. "No—now that the Population Police are in charge, it'd be like looking for a needle in a *burning* haystack."

"Oh, I've done that," Mark said airily. "It's a game we used to play, after we got rid of all our livestock and didn't need our hay no more. You throw a match into the haystack, give the fire a three-second head start, and begin looking. You can find the needle every time if you work quick."

Trey couldn't do anything but stare at the other boy. Mark wasn't just crazily brave—he was stark, raving mad. Trey thought longingly of his cozy cupboard hiding place back in the Talbots' kitchen. He could be back there in a matter of minutes. He certainly wasn't spending any more time hanging around this lunatic.

But Smits stepped forward.

"You'll help Mark, won't you, Trey?" he said. "If the two of you work together, I know you can get to Lee. You'll rescue him, won't you?"

It's impossible, Trey thought. *It's ridiculous to risk two more lives when we've got no chance of success. This is insanity. It's a suicide mission!* He thought about how deluded Smits was, thinking Trey had ever been able to protect anybody, thinking Trey might be able to take care of somebody else, instead of needing somebody to take care of him.

That one time I saved Lee's life, it was a fluke, you know? he wanted to scream at Smits. *I can't do anything. I'm a coward!*

But what he said to Smits was: "Yes."

CHAPTER *TEN*

O kay. Ready to go?" Mark asked.

"Now?" Trey squeaked. He wanted more ceremony somehow—a commissioning service, perhaps, or an anointing of the heroes, like he'd read about in books. Some acknowledgment that brave men (okay—boys) were about to head into danger.

Or maybe he just wanted a delay. A chance to change his mind.

"What—you want to wait until the Population Police make it a crime to go anywhere? Of course now!" Mark said.

Trey could feel Smits's eyes on him.

"P-papers," Trey managed to stammer. "We've got to take the papers from the Talbots' house first."

He didn't know why that seemed so important suddenly, except that he'd brought papers to the Talbots' and it didn't seem right to leave them behind.

"The Talbots? They're the ones in the big house over there?" Mark asked, pointing.

Trey felt so disoriented that he barely could have identified up from down, but he nodded.

Mark shrugged. "Always wanted to see inside one of those monster houses," he said.

And Trey was glad, because he wasn't sure he could muster enough courage to go back into the Talbots' house alone, then leave again, if he was also supposed to be gathering courage to go rescue Lee.

Mark extinguished the lantern, and they stepped from the dark of the barn into the dark of the night. Mark led the way, holding branches back so Trey had a clear path. They were halfway to the Talbots' house before Trey realized Smits hadn't followed.

"Shouldn't we wait for Smits—I mean, Peter?" Trey asked.

"I sent him to bed," Mark said. "He's just a little kid."

He's a Baron, Trey thought. *He's used to other people doing his dirty work for him.*

What if Trey adopted that attitude? What if he just sent Mark out alone to rescue Lee?

It was a tempting thought.

They reached the door of the Talbots' house, and Mark hesitated for the first time.

"They don't have any of those fancy alarms on this, do they?" he asked.

"I just walked out this door fifteen minutes ago," Trey said. "No alarms went off then. The electricity's out, anyway. What are you, scared?"

Trey enjoyed taunting Mark, but his bravado was false. For all Trey knew, there could be silent alarms rigged up on the door, ones that secretly alerted the police even without electricity. Would that kind of an alarm be battery-operated, or would the Talbots have needed a backup generator? If they had a backup generator, wouldn't the lights have stayed on in their house even when the rest of the neighborhood lost power? What if it was all a trick?

While Trey was still considering every possibility, Mark shrugged and stepped into the Talbots' house. Nothing happened. Feeling sheepish, Trey followed.

"Draw the shades, and I'll light the lantern again," Mark said.

Trey pulled blinds down over the window he'd used for spying, and jerked curtains along a rod to cover the sliding door they'd just walked in through. Then Mark struck a match and lit the lantern. His jaw dropped and his eyes widened.

"Those Barons must have lived like pigs," he said, surveying the mess before him.

"Their house was searched, remember?" Trey said. "Fifty guys in uniforms trashed it. I bet this house was a showplace before."

He didn't know why he felt compelled to defend the Talbots. He just didn't like the note of glee in Mark's voice.

"Well, get your papers, then," Mark said.

Trey had hidden them in the kitchen cupboard. He

retrieved them and, straightening up, saw the avalanche of papers covering the counters.

"I should take those, too," he said. The thought had just occurred to him. He hadn't read any of them, and they were probably worthless, since the uniformed men hadn't carted them off and Mrs. Talbot apparently hadn't wanted them either. But it seemed wrong, suddenly, to leave them behind. Trey's father had taught him that nothing was more valuable than the printed word, and Trey couldn't shake that belief now.

Mark didn't seem to be listening.

"So much food," he muttered, looking at the boxes and bags strewn about the kitchen. "It was true, then: They even had more food than we did—and we were the ones growing it."

"All that food's not doing the Talbots any good now," Trey said.

Mark squinted, and the dim light from the lantern turned each squint line into a deep shadow.

"S'pose it would be stealing to take some of it?" Mark asked. "Just in case, I mean—if we're going to be gone a while. . . ."

Trey didn't like thinking about how long they might be gone. He didn't even like thinking about the fact that they were going anywhere.

"Mrs. Talbot said other people were welcome to anything in this house," he said, trying to shrug casually. "She left it all behind and didn't care."

"Anything?" Mark asked, his eyes big.

In the end, they took only some food and the papers, and bags to carry it all in. But after they'd stepped out into the darkness again, Mark kept casting longing glances back at the house.

"Bet it'll all be gone before I get home," he muttered regretfully.

Trey was more convinced than ever that Mark was a lunatic.

They loaded everything into a mud-covered pickup truck back in the scary barn. Mark stuffed the papers into a slit in the seat—"Just in case we get stopped," he muttered. The food from the Talbots' house went into battered bushel baskets in the back. Mark covered the top of each basket with a layer of moldy-looking potatoes.

He was admiring his work when someone pounded on the door of the barn. In a flash, Trey dived under the truck.

"Mark!" a voice called from outside. "Mother says you've got to come in to bed now."

"Just a minute," Mark called back.

From his hiding place under the truck, Trey could see the door open. Another boy stepped into the barn.

"What you doing out here anyway?" the boy asked.

"Loading the truck for Dad to take to town. So's he can take the potatoes to market," Mark said. Trey was amazed at how calm Mark sounded, how even he kept his voice, how easily he lied.

The other boy snorted.

"Dad ain't going to town," he said. "The way things are going, Dad ain't never leaving home again. And neither are we."

"You've been sneaking out to see Becky," Mark said. "You're risking your life to go visit your stupid, ugly girl-friend."

The other boy didn't deny it. He didn't even defend his girlfriend. Trey couldn't see anything of him but his bare feet. The feet shifted awkwardly.

"So?" the boy said.

"So what do you see when you go?" Mark asked. His voice was low now, almost hypnotic. "You seen any soldiers or anything? Policemen? Anybody tried to stop you?"

"I walk four miles there and four miles back, from Becky's house," the other boy said. "Through the corn-fields. Ain't no soldiers or policemen hiding out in the *cornfields.*"

"Oh," Mark said, almost sounding disappointed that the other boy hadn't run into dozens of police officers, scads of soldiers. Mark, Trey decided, was smarter than he looked. He was trying to prepare for his trip by pumping the boy for information.

But Mark and Trey wouldn't be able to walk through cornfields to get to the Grants' house.

"Don't you go tattling on me," the other boy warned.

"I won't," Mark said.

Apparently satisfied, the boy walked out of the barn.

Mark bent down and whispered to Trey.

"I've got to go in now. Matthew—my brother—he'd tell Mother and Dad if I didn't. We need some sleep anyhow. I'll come back at dawn and then—and then . . ."

"And then we leave," Trey whispered back.

"Reckon so," Mark said roughly. In the shadows, Trey could barely see his face. "I'm sorry I can't invite you into the house so . . . you know. You'll be okay out here, won't you? You won't—won't go nowhere or nothing, will you?"

"Where would I go?" Trey asked.

And then Mark went away, taking the light with him. In the dark, Trey twisted around uncomfortably on the hard packed-dirt floor.

I should have told Mark I'd go back and sleep at the Talbots' house and he could come and get me there in the morning. I could have slept in the lap of luxury tonight, instead of on dirt.

But the Talbots' house seemed scarier than ever now. He'd seen the gleam of greed in Mark's eye when Trey had said that Mrs. Talbot had abandoned all her possessions and didn't care about getting them back. There had to be dozens of others, even greedier, who wanted what the Talbots had had. Trey could close his eyes and imagine hordes descending upon the Talbots' house: boys in flannel shirts, like Mark; men in uniform, like the Population Police; new Government bureaucrats in suits and ties.

And Trey was afraid of them all.

CHAPTER *ELEVEN*

It felt like the middle of the night when Mark was back, shaking Trey by the shoulders.

"Here, put this on," Mark muttered.

Groggily Trey accepted a flannel shirt, thick with quilting—almost a jacket, really. He wrapped it around his shoulders. It *was* warmer, and Trey was a little touched that Mark had thought to share. Trey was still wearing the formal servant clothes he'd been wearing the night of the Grants' fatal party: stiff black pants, a thin, white cotton shirt. Except that the white shirt wasn't exactly white anymore, not after days of hiding out at the Talbots' and, now, sleeping on a dirt floor.

"Watch your head," Mark said gruffly as Trey rolled out from under the truck.

Mark opened the driver's side door, and the light that glowed suddenly inside the truck's cab seemed almost blinding.

"Better button that up," Mark said, and Trey blinked in

confusion. Button a light? A door? A truck? "The *shirt*," Mark said impatiently.

Red-faced, Trey forced his clumsy fingers to prod buttons through buttonholes. Then he slipped into the seat of the truck, even though it felt like climbing into a spotlight. He slid as far away from the light as possible, and huddled against the far door.

"Let's go then," Mark said.

Trey glanced around and saw that Mark had opened a huge door behind the truck, leading out of the barn. A gigantic portion of the starry sky seemed to stare back at him.

"No, wait," Mark said. "Let's push it out to the road." Trey just stared at him. "So nobody hears."

It seemed to take Mark forever to explain in a way Trey could understand: Trey would have to get out of the truck, then stand at the front of the truck and shove on the hood as hard as he could, until the truck rolled out to the road.

"I can't," Trey whimpered.

Mark stared at him for a minute, then said, "Fine. You steer. I'll push."

And then Mark practically had to give him an entire driving lesson: "Turn the wheel slowly. . . . No, no, don't look straight ahead, look out the back window—"

"Why?" Trey said. "Why does the seat face forward if I'm supposed to be looking backward?"

"Because we're going in reverse," Mark said disgustedly.

Trey wondered how much it would take for Mark to

give up on him, to just snort, "Fine! You stay here! I'll go rescue my brother by myself!"

Is that what I really want? Trey wondered.

It was yet another question he didn't want to think about.

Finally Mark seemed satisfied that Trey could steer the truck properly. Mark put the truck in neutral, and moved around to the front.

Mark was strong. It seemed like no time at all before he'd pushed the truck to the edge of the gravel driveway. Then he went back to shut the barn door while Trey cowered in the truck.

"Think *you're* going to drive the whole way?" Mark asked when he came back.

"What? Oh," Trey said, and he slid over away from the steering wheel.

Mark climbed in and shut the door. He turned the key, and the engine coughed a few times, then sputtered to life. The sound seemed as loud as a jumbo jet roaring through the night sky. Trey was certain that the racket would wake not just Mark's family, but the entire countryside.

Mark didn't seem worried, though. He just patted the dashboard and muttered, "Good old Bessie."

Trey squeezed his eyes shut in terror. What was he thinking? How could he be doing this? Why go looking for danger?

Beside him, Mark started whistling. Whistling!

Trey opened his eyes a crack. The dashboard glowed

with dials and numbers. Beyond, the truck's headlights sliced into the solid darkness around them.

"Why didn't you tell your family?" Trey asked Mark softly. "How could you just—" He almost said "abandon them," but stopped himself at the last minute. "How could you just leave without letting them know where you were going?"

Mark glanced quickly over at Trey, then focused his eyes on the road again.

"They'd worry," he said.

"And they're not going to worry now? With you disappearing?" Trey asked incredulously.

"They'll think I'm just running around. Carousing. Getting in trouble." Mark hesitated. "Little trouble, not big trouble."

Trey didn't want any trouble, of any size. Had Mark done this kind of thing before—taking his family's truck out in the middle of the night, going who-knows-where? Did they expect it of him? What was Trey thinking, casting his lot with a troublemaker?

"Uh-oh," Mark muttered.

"What?" Trey asked, panicked.

Mark didn't answer, just pointed at a pair of headlights far down the road, coming right at them.

CHAPTER TWELVE

urn onto a side street! Hide!" Trey screamed. Without thinking, he grabbed for the steering wheel. Mark shoved him away with one hand, as easily as he might brush aside a fly.

"Ain't another road for miles," Mark said. "Want to end up in the ditch? Just wait—"

The headlights drew closer. Mark seemed to be speeding up, and Trey had a moment of insane hope. How fast would the truck have to be going to just jump over whatever vehicle—whatever danger—was coming their way?

But that was childish thinking, based on a comic book his mother had let him read once when his father thought he was studying Latin. Real trucks couldn't jump.

"Hmm," Mark murmured. "It's old Hobart."

"Who?" Trey asked.

Mark put his foot on the brake.

"What are you doing?" Trey screamed.

"Shh," Mark said.

The truck slowed, then stopped, as the other vehicle—another pickup—drew alongside them. Trey could only stare in paralyzed horror as Mark began slowly rolling down his window. The other driver did the same.

"Hey," Mark said.

"Hey," the other driver said. In the near-dark, Trey could tell only that it was an old man. His grizzled white hair and beard glowed eerily in the green light of the dashboard.

"Whozat you got with you?" the old man asked.

"My cousin," Mark said calmly. "He was here visiting when—you know. Hobart, this is Silas. Silas, this is Hobart."

Trey guessed he was supposed to be Silas. He nodded awkwardly, even though it was probably too dark for Hobart to notice. Trey was glad of the darkness. It'd make it impossible for Hobart to ever say exactly whom he'd seen.

"Now, I'm so old, it don't matter no more what happens to me," Hobart said. "That's why my family sent *me* to town to see if we got any money left in the bank. But, a couple of young scamps like yourselves—where are you off to in such a hurry that it's worth risking your life to go there?"

Trey held his breath. Mark wouldn't dare answer that question, would he?

"I'm not driving that fast," Mark said.

Hobart chuckled. It was a grim sound in the dark.

"Fast, slow, it don't matter. These days, leaving your house is like asking to be killed. I heard tell they was shooting anyone who even tried to drive into Boginsville. And over in Farlee, they've got soldiers patrolling the streets, telling people to turn out their lights, or turn on their lights, or cook them supper, or dance walking upside down on their hands—whatever the soldiers want, the soldiers get, or else they pull the trigger. And sometimes, they pull the trigger just for fun, no matter what the people do," Hobart said. "Best thing you two could do is just turn right around and go on home."

Trey gulped and waited for Mark to answer.

"Looks like *you* survived, being out," Mark said.

"Soldiers haven't made it out to Hurleyton," Hobart said. "Yet."

"Was the bank open?" Mark asked. Even Trey, who could never detect subtle innuendo in any conversation, could tell that Mark wasn't just making idle chitchat.

"Nah," Hobart said. "Whole town's shut down tight."

"It generally is at five in the morning," Mark said.

"You questioning my story, boy?" Hobart growled. "I came out yesterday afternoon. When I couldn't get into the bank, I spent the night at my nephew's house in town."

"Playing cards and gambling and drinking," Mark said.

"So? They haven't made that illegal yet too, have they?" Hobart practically whined.

"They will if your wife starts telling the soldiers what to do," Mark said.

Hobart laughed, and Trey was surprised. Hobart and Mark had seemed to be on the verge of an argument, but suddenly it was like they were best friends sharing a private joke.

"Tell you what, boy," Hobart said. "You don't tell no one you seen me, I won't tell no one I seen you."

"Deal," Mark said.

"Okay, then," Hobart said. But he didn't drive away yet. He peered straight at Mark and Trey, and for a second Trey was certain that the old man's glittering eyes had taken in the contrast between Trey's flannel shirt and his stiff servant pants. Trey even feared that the old man could see through the dusty seat to the papers Trey had taken from the Grants' and the Talbots' houses.

"I don't know what you two are up to," Hobart said. "But you be careful now, you hear? Don't do nothing I wouldn't do."

"Well now, that don't restrict us much, does it?" Mark teased back.

Hobart chuckled and began rolling his window up. Slowly, he drove on.

Trey let out a deep breath. He felt dizzy—now that he thought about it, he wasn't sure he'd let himself breathe the whole time Mark had been talking to Hobart.

Mark was rolling up his window now, too, and expertly shifting gears to get the truck going faster and faster.

"Can we trust Hobart?" Trey asked in a small voice that seemed to get lost in the sound of the truck's engine. He was trying to decide if the question was worth repeating, when Mark answered.

"Hobart's terrible about cheating at cards," Mark said. "But if he says he won't tell nobody about us, he won't."

And Trey wasn't sure whether to be relieved or disappointed. If Hobart had insisted on telling Mark's parents—maybe even dragged Mark and Trey straight back to Mark's house—their dangerous journey would be over practically before it started. Trey could have said, "Oh, well, we tried," and given up with a clear conscience.

But the way it was now, he felt guilty for wanting to quit.

And he was still heading straight into danger.

MARGARET PETERSON HADDIX

CHAPTER *THIRTEEN*

The Grants' house was on the outskirts of a huge city miles and miles away from the Talbots' mansion and Mark's family's farm. That meant Trey had hours of sitting in the pickup truck, regretting every revolution of the wheels beneath him.

Mark provided no conversation to distract him. Trey wondered if the fear was catching up with Mark as well, because his face seemed to grow paler and paler the farther they went; his skin seemed to stretch tighter and tighter across the bones of his face.

At least they saw no other vehicles after Hobart's. Indeed, the landscapes they traveled through seemed utterly deserted, utterly devoid of any signs of life. Trey wondered if Hobart's tales of soldiers everywhere were mere figments of his imagination; he wondered if the news reports of riots were lies as well. Riots required people, and there appeared to be no people anywhere.

Finally, when Trey had lost all track of time, and all

sense of how long they'd been traveling and how much farther they had to go, Mark suddenly veered off the road.

"Wha—Mark! Wake up! You're driving crazy!" Trey screamed, convinced that Mark had fallen into a trance of sorts as well.

"I'm going this way on purpose, stupid," Mark hissed through clenched teeth as he steered the truck down a steep dirt slope. A river lay directly ahead.

Trey clutched the dashboard and squeezed his eyes shut. This wasn't the way he'd expected to die.

The truck stopped suddenly. Trey hadn't felt any dramatic leap over the riverbank, and he felt no water lapping at his feet, so he dared to look again.

They'd stopped in a small woods. All he could see through the windshield now were thick branches and leaves, jarringly red and orange and yellow.

"Has there been some sort of nuclear contamination here?" Trey asked.

"Huh?" Mark said.

"The leaves," Trey said. "They're—not green. Is there radiation? Is it safe?"

Mark's jaw dropped, ever so slightly.

"It's October," he said. "Fall. Didn't nobody never tell you that leaves change colors in the fall? Didn't you ever notice?"

"Oh," Trey said. He remembered now. He'd seen pictures in books, of course, but the autumn leaves had never looked so bright and gaudy in pictures. "I was never outside until last December," he said defensively.

Mark was staring at him.

"Let me get this straight," he said. "You never once stepped foot outdoors until last year?"

"No," Trey said.

"Didn't you ever even peek out a window?"

"No. It was too dangerous."

Mark's jaw was practically dragging the floor of the truck now, he looked so stunned.

"I think . . . ," he started. "I think if I'd never seen the outdoors, I'd keep my eyes open once I was in it."

"I do!" Trey said.

"No you don't. You had your eyes closed practically the whole way here."

"No I didn't!"

"Yes you did! I bet we passed dozens of trees with turned leaves. Why didn't you ask if any of them was contaminated?"

Now that Trey thought about it, he remembered a few swirls of colors along the way. But he wasn't going to admit to Mark that his way of looking out windows was mostly by way of quick, fearful glances. He *had* kept his eyes open, but he'd mainly been looking at the dashboard.

"Never mind," Mark said suddenly, in a rough voice. "It don't matter." He drummed his fingers on the steering wheel. "I was thinking, we're almost there. If we hide the truck here and go the rest of the way on foot, we won't stick out so much."

"We don't want to be conspicuous," Trey agreed. So he didn't know anything about trees and leaves—so what. At least he could supply Mark with a better word than "stick out so much."

"Uh, yeah," Mark said. "I have maps for getting over close to the city, and Peter—Smits . . . whatever you want to call him—he told me where his house was. So I know where to go. But, um . . ."

Trey waited, but Mark didn't seem inclined to keep talking. He just sat there, staring out the windshield at the branches and brilliant leaves.

"What?" Trey prompted.

"We was on back roads up till now," Mark said. "I avoided every single bit of civilization I could. But now . . . I ain't never been in a city. Is there anything I should know? So I don't make any mistakes, I mean?"

Trey looked at Mark, in his flannel shirt, faded jeans, and heavy work boots. Under his dusty cap, Mark's face held a mix of fear and hope. He looked like he really thought Trey could give him good advice.

"I don't know," Trey said. He'd grown up in a city, of course, but what had he ever seen of it? "Just don't say 'ain't' anymore, okay?"

"Uh, okay," Mark said, but he looked like Trey had slapped him. Trey wanted to take his words back. They were two ignoramuses going into danger they couldn't even imagine. What did a little strangled grammar matter?

Mark shoved his door open, banging it on a tree branch.

"Help me cover the rest of the truck so nobody sees it from the road," he said gruffly.

Following Mark's instructions, Trey broke off branches to drape over the back of the pickup, where it stuck out the most. Even Trey could hear the edge in Mark's voice as he patiently told him that everything Trey tried to do was wrong.

"No, Trey, you can't break off a ten-inch-thick branch with your bare hands—you'd need a saw for that. . . ."

"No, Trey, if we just pull off a leaf or two at a time, this is going to take hours. . . ."

When Mark was finally satisfied that the truck was hidden well enough—even creeping back up to the road to see for himself—he and Trey got out some of the food they'd taken from the Talbots' house and sat down in the brush to eat.

"Eat the heaviest stuff first," Mark told him. "We'll carry the lighter food with us."

And then Trey had to compare. Was a banana heavier than a peach? Was a bag of peanuts heavier than a box of raisins? Mark watched him in disgust.

"Just eat whatever you want," Mark said. "We're strong enough to carry it all. Or—I am."

Trey wanted to say, "Why are you bringing me along? What good am I if you don't even think I can carry a knapsack?" But he swallowed his words, along with the peanuts. Both stuck in his throat.

Their meal was a quick affair. In a matter of minutes,

Mark was on his feet again, pouring food into the knapsack. Trey climbed back into the cab of the truck and pulled out the papers he'd taken from first the Grants' house, then the Talbots'.

"Put these in there too," he said.

Mark hesitated.

"I don't know," he said. "If anybody stops us—if they search our bag . . ."

Trey knew what Mark meant. The papers could make them look like thieves. How could he explain where he'd gotten them? But the papers were all he had left. He had nothing from his life with his parents, nothing from his life at Hendricks. The papers were the only link he had to any point in his life when anyone cared about him.

"I'll carry them myself then," Trey said. He stuffed the most important Grant papers—and a few of the Talbots' papers he'd grabbed blindly—into an inside pocket of his flannel shirt. He wanted to take everything, but it wouldn't fit without bulging. He knew he couldn't push his luck too far. He shoved the leftover papers back into the slit in the seat.

Mark's eyes looked troubled, but he didn't object. He turned away and rearranged the branches over the truck one last time.

"I thought we could walk along the river," Mark said quietly. "If we're lucky, there'll be trees the whole way."

Trey nodded, but panic clutched him. They were leaving the truck behind. For all Trey knew, the Grants' house might still be miles away. Did Mark really expect Trey to walk that far *outdoors?* And once they arrived, they had no guarantee whatsoever that Lee would be there too.

"Are you sure this is the best way?" Trey asked. "What if—what if the phones are working now? Shouldn't we at least check?"

"You see anyone standing around offering us a free call?" Mark asked mockingly. "Would you trust anyone who did?"

"No," Trey whispered.

Mark turned and started off walking. Trey scrambled to keep up.

Walking, Trey found, was possible as long as he stayed right behind Mark. He kept his eyes on the gray plaid of Mark's flannel shirt, and didn't look up or down or side to side. This made Trey stumble every so often, and he probably looked like a total fool, always lifting his feet too high, just in case there were any logs or undergrowth in his path. But Mark didn't say anything about it, just looked around every now and then to make sure Trey was still nearby.

After they'd gone a few yards, Mark whispered back over his shoulder, "Down!" When Trey didn't respond right away, Mark grabbed him by the arm and jerked him toward the ground. Trey lay flat, his right ear pressed hard into the dirt. Was he hearing tramping feet or just the beating of his own heart?

"We'll crawl from here on out," Mark whispered.

Trey didn't ask why, just silently panicked. How could he keep his eyes on Mark's shirt if they were crawling?

Mark was already sliding away from him. The toe of Mark's boot disappeared over the edge of a branch, and suddenly Mark was out of sight. Trey was alone again.

"Wait!" Trey whispered urgently, and dived over the branch.

Mark was right there, waiting in a hollow of dirt and leaves. Silently he started moving once more, and Trey followed, terrified of losing sight of Mark again.

What they were doing couldn't properly be called "crawling." It was more like slithering. Mark had the grace of a snake, slipping unseen through the brush. Trey broke branches and crunched leaves. An elephant, he thought, could not have been any louder or clumsier.

Hey, Dad? Trey thought. *Why was it more important to learn Latin than this?*

But Trey knew. His father had never thought that Trey would ever have to move anything but his eyes as they flicked across lines of print, or his fingertips as they turned the pages of a book.

Why? Trey thought. *If you knew I wasn't going to hide forever—*

That was too close to dangerous thoughts, thoughts he never wanted to think again. He forced himself to concentrate on keeping up with Mark.

After what seemed like hours—or maybe even days— Mark stopped in the midst of a small clearing. He crouched beside Trey and pointed, whispering, "Is that it?"

Trey looked up, even though it was scary to gaze straight toward the sky. The peak of a roof rose just above the tops of the tallest trees. A cupola soared above the roof. Squinting, Trey could just barely make out a stylized "G" in gold on the pinnacle of the cupola. Was it "G" for "Grant"?

"Maybe," Trey whispered back.

Mark nodded and started crawling again.

"They have a fence, I think," Trey said, straining to remember. He'd arrived at the Grants' in a car that had whisked him through . . . was it a gate? He hadn't been paying attention. He'd been too busy worrying.

"I know," Mark said. "Peter told me everything."

Trey had to struggle to remember that Mark meant Smits, that Peter was Smits. Then he had to struggle to catch up with Mark before he disappeared behind a tree. When Trey caught up, Mark was still talking.

"The fence goes all around the entire property, but it's stone, and at the back, closest to the river, there's a place where a stone comes out, just wide enough for a boy to squeeze through. Peter and his brother used to sneak out that way. . . ."

Trey was glad that Mark knew so much. He'd known to hide the truck, he'd known to follow the river to the Grants' house, and now he knew exactly how to get in. Really, Trey had nothing to worry about as long as he stuck close to Mark.

Then Mark stopped in front of him, so abruptly that Trey's nose slammed right into the bottom of Mark's shoe.

"Listen," Mark hissed over his shoulder.

A booming voice echoed through the woods. At first Trey couldn't make out any words, but as he crept forward a little, the voice got louder: "There! And there! Faster!" it screamed in the distance.

Trey looked at Mark, but his face was wrinkled up in puzzlement too.

"Should we turn around?" Trey asked, sotto voce.

Mark shook his head.

"Just be very, very quiet," he said, so softly that Trey practically had to lip-read.

They inched forward at an excruciatingly slow pace. The voice was even louder now.

"Come on, men! You think you're going to get paid for such shoddy work? I've never seen such a bunch of lazy, good-for-nothing louts! Move it!"

They could hear hammering, too, and grunts of pain or exertion. Trey couldn't figure out why Mark thought they should be so quiet: Nobody would be able to hear a few boys creeping through the forest in the midst of all that racket.

Trey saw the stone wall first. He was so relieved they wouldn't have to creep past the voice and the hammerers that he couldn't speak. He tugged at Mark's sleeve and pointed.

But Mark shook his head warningly. He led Trey along

the wall, closer and closer to the noise.

They rounded a curve in the wall, and Mark suddenly jerked Trey behind a big bush.

"There," he mouthed.

Terrified, Trey peeked through the leaves. All along the stone fence ahead of them, a team of gray-uniformed men—forty? fifty? a hundred?—were driving stakes in the ground and nailing long strands of wire to the stakes.

"Why," Mark whispered, "would they need a stone fence and a barbed-wire fence too?"

Trey shrugged, totally confused. Why would anyone build a new fence around the Grants' house after Mr. and Mrs. Grant had died? Who had authorized it? Lee? The chauffeur?

"Let's just climb through the hole in the stone fence," Trey begged. "Quick. Before they see us."

"Can't," Mark whispered back. "The hole's over there."

And he pointed straight into the midst of the uniformed men.

CHAPTER *FOURTEEN*

B y silent agreement, Trey and Mark crept deeper into the woods to figure out what to do next. Trey was all for waiting until the team of workers left—maybe even rethinking the entire mission.

"What if there's a better way to help Lee than climbing through two fences?" he said. "Let's both think for a while, talk it out. . . . Maybe we've been overlooking an obvious solution. Maybe we don't even need to step foot on the Grants' property at all."

The more he thought about it, the more the second fence spooked him. It just didn't fit.

"You want to sit around thinking and talking?" Mark asked incredulously. "Doing nothing? It could be hours before those men leave. And during those hours, my brother could be—"

Trey didn't want to hear how Mark finished that sentence.

"So what do *you* want to do?" he challenged.

88   MARGARET PETERSON HADDIX

"Let's go around that way and see if there's another way in," he said, pointing in the opposite direction from the men assembling the barbed-wire fence. "Maybe the front gate's open."

Trey couldn't believe Mark thought they might be able to just stroll right in, in broad daylight. But Mark wasn't waiting for Trey to continue the debate. He was already moving gingerly through the underbrush, away from Trey.

Silently fuming, Trey followed.

By the time they reached the edge of the woods, every muscle in Trey's body ached. He just wasn't used to lifting his feet so carefully, then placing them down again so precisely that no twigs cracked, no leaves rustled. Really, he wasn't very accustomed to moving his feet at all. And it wasn't just his feet and legs—his arms ached from shoving away branch after branch. His back ached from crouching. He'd scraped one hand on the rough stone of the wall, and the other on a thorny plant he hadn't noticed until it scratched him. He was in such a fog of pain and exhaustion that he didn't even mind seeing the patch of clear sky up ahead. What more could the horrible outdoors do to him?

It was Mark who stopped him from stepping out into the clearing.

"Wait," he whispered, grabbing Trey's arm. "Look."

Once again, Trey peered through leaves. He blinked twice, sure his eyes were fooling him. There, on the driveway leading to the gate of the Grant estate, stood hundreds of men and boys, lined up and waiting patiently for . . . what? And why hadn't he and Mark heard them? How could so many people be so quiet?

Then Trey noticed that none of them were talking. Or, no—a few were, but whispering, their heads bent close together, their voices low. It was like they were as scared of being overheard as he and Mark were.

"What do you reckon they're doing here?" Mark asked.

Trey just shook his head. Mark looked disappointed, as if he'd thought this huge crowd was some city phenomenon that Trey would understand and explain instantly.

"I'm going to go ask one of them," Mark said.

"No!" Trey exploded. "They might—"

"What?" Mark asked. "What's the worst thing anyone could do to me, just for asking a question?"

"Kill you," Trey argued quietly.

Mark rolled his eyes.

"Help me," he said. "Let's pick the right person."

As far as Trey was concerned, one person standing in a line was pretty much the same as any other. But he obediently peered through the leaves again. Everyone in the line was dressed in ragged clothes; everyone was thin, with a gaunt face. But, looking closely, Trey could see some differences. Some of the boys were young—his age, maybe even younger—and they had the most hopeful expressions. Some of them even looked like they thought they might be embarking on an adventure. The oldest men in the crowd, though, had dead-looking eyes and vacant gazes. Some of them looked like they really might kill someone for asking a question. Or maybe they thought they were about to be killed themselves.

"That one," Mark said suddenly.

He pointed at a boy about his age. Trey knew instantly why Mark had chosen him. He was wearing the same kind of flannel shirt as Mark and Trey.

"You shouldn't—you can't—," Trey sputtered.

But Mark was already stepping out of the brush, walking toward the line.

Trey peered fearfully after him. He clutched the trunk of the tree beside him so tightly that bark came off in his hands.

Mark's walk was almost a saunter. At first, no one from the line even glanced at him. Then, as he reached the edge of the blacktop, a few boys raised their eyes in his direction. One was the boy in the flannel shirt.

"Hey," Mark said. "What's this line for?"

Flannel-shirt boy looked around desperately, side to side, as if he was hoping that Mark was speaking to someone else—was drawing attention to someone else. But then he answered. Trey could see his mouth moving, even though Trey couldn't hear a single word he said.

Mark moved in closer to flannel-shirt boy. Mark had his back to Trey now, but Trey could tell by the way he turned his head that he was talking now too, just so softly that Trey couldn't hear. Mark and flannel-shirt boy were having a regular conversation, back and forth and back and forth. They were both intense. Once, flannel-shirt boy frowned at something Mark said, then cupped his hand over Mark's ear, whispering so no one else could hear.

After a few minutes, Mark walked back into the woods.

"What?" Trey asked as soon as Mark was close enough. "What are they doing?"

"They're waiting in line to join Population Police forces," Mark said.

"What?" Trey said. He looked again at the long, long line, and held back a shiver. "At the Grants' house? What do the Grants have to do with the Population Police?"

Mark was peering out at the line too. But his eyes didn't seem to be focusing.

"It's not the Grants' house anymore," he said. "It belongs to the Population Police now. In fact—it's their new headquarters."

CHAPTER *FIFTEEN*

rey jerked back, like he actually thought he could get away from this horrible news Mark had just revealed. "No," he moaned.

"Maybe that kid's lying," Mark said tonelessly. "But I don't know. Why would he lie?"

Trey realized he was trembling. He tried to stop, to regain control of his muscles, but it was useless. He was mere yards away from the headquarters of the Population Police, the people who had wanted to kill Trey ever since he was born. He had every right to tremble.

Without thinking about it, he plunged his hand into his pants pocket and clutched the false identity card his mother had given him after his father died. He'd carried it with him ever since. It was his only protection against certain death.

"Trey?" Mark said. "Maybe my brother's not in there. Maybe he and his friends—your friends—maybe they escaped before the Population Police took over."

Mark thought Trey was trembling on Lee's behalf. Mark thought Trey was only worried about his friends.

"Maybe the chauffeur who took Lee was working for the Population Police the whole time," Trey said, and was instantly ashamed. Why was he trying to upset Mark?

"We've got to find him," Mark said.

But he didn't suggest a plan, just stared dully out at the line of new recruits for the Population Police.

Trey couldn't help staring at the line too, even though it terrified him. He couldn't see the line's beginning or its end. It seemed to go on forever, all those men and boys.

"That many people want to work for the Population Police?" Trey whimpered. "Do they all hate third children so much? Does everyone?"

"No," Mark said, finally looking away from the line. "They probably don't know anything about third children. They're just hungry."

"So what? Who isn't?" Trey asked.

Mark sighed.

"Apparently the Population Police announced this morning that nobody can sell food now except the Population Police," he said. "And nobody can buy food unless at least one person in the family works for the Population Police. So everybody's joining up. So they don't starve."

Trey closed his eyes, suddenly feeling dizzy with hunger himself. Or maybe it was just fear again. He'd been so terrified for so long, he would have thought he'd be numb to the emotion by now. But he wasn't. Fear seemed to have taken control of every nerve ending in his body. He couldn't quite make sense of what Mark had said. If the Population Police controlled the food supply . . . If everybody joined the Population Police . . .

He was doomed. So was every other third child. So was the entire country.

"Listen," Mark was saying. "I—I told that kid I had food to sell. I told him he didn't have to join the Population Police. I don't know, I guess I went a little crazy. I was even telling him how to grow food. . . ."

Mark's words took a while to sink in.

"What?" Trey asked. "What if he turns you in? What if the Population Police are offering a big reward for turning in people who try to sell food illegally, just like they offer rewards for turning in third children?"

Trey didn't wait for Mark to answer. He grabbed Mark's arm and began tugging.

"We've got to hide!" Trey screamed frantically. "Now!"

Blindly he crashed back through the woods, pulling Mark along with him.

"Trey! Shh! You're—someone's going to hear us!" Mark hollered.

Trey stopped with a jerk—not because of Mark's protests, but because eight lines of barbed wire stretched directly in front of him. He'd thought he'd been running deeper and deeper into the woods, but in his panic he must have gone in circles. He was back at the dual fences surrounding the Grant estate.

He and Mark stared in silence at the gleaming silver barbed wire. Then Mark whispered, "They're gone now."

"Huh?" Trey said. He was a little mesmerized by the barbed wire. One barb was suspended mere inches from his right eye. What if he hadn't seen it? What if he hadn't stopped?

"The workers," Mark said impatiently. "They finished up and left. So . . ." He took one small step closer to the fence.

Trey snapped out of his trance.

"You still want to crawl through?" he hissed. "You've got to be kidding! It's not safe! Not with the Population Police in there now. Look, Mark, I know you're brave and all, but—you can't save Lee!"

"I have to try," Mark said quietly.

"You won't even make it through the barbed wire," Trey argued frantically.

"Sure I will," Mark said. "Don't you know how many barbed-wire fences I've crawled through in my life? I'm practically the barbed-wire champion. Ain't never—I mean, haven't never—gotten a scratch since I was about three years old!"

Trey didn't bother telling him his grammar was atrocious, even without the "ain't." Mark wasn't waiting for Trey's approval anyway. He took another step forward, past Trey.

"Just watch," Mark said, a daredevil grin plastered across his face.

He took off his knapsack and tossed it aside. Then he eased his right foot between two of the lowest lines of barbed wire. Neither wire touched his leg. Trey took a step back so he could see better as Mark crouched down and began moving the rest of his body through. With one hand, he reached for the wire above to hold it away from his head.

"Aaahh!" Mark screamed. He dropped the wire, and it bounced against the entire length of his back. He jerked away, his voice cut off mid-scream. But he was still caught in the fence. His body sagged against the bottom wire.

Without thinking, Trey grabbed a stick and poked at Mark's body, knocking him off the wire. The stick brushed the fence, and Trey's wrists and knuckles tingled strangely. He dropped the stick and jumped back, totally panicked. He'd been crazy to use a stick damp from the ground. Water conducted electricity. And the barbed-wire fence, he realized, had been electrified with dangerous amounts of voltage. He stared at Mark's motionless body, sprawled on the other side of the fence. Trey wasn't even sure that Mark was still alive.

Above them, on the original stone fence, a light suddenly clicked on, flooding the entire area with an intense glow. Frantically, Trey scuttled backward, desperately searching for shadows to hide in. Seconds later, he heard the sound of marching feet, coming right toward him. He dove into a bush, breaking branches. Trembling, he reached back to steady the leaves, to hide all signs of his frantic dive.

"Intruder discovered in second quadrant," a man's voice boomed nearby.

Trey dared to peek out through the leaves. Four men in uniform were standing beside the barbed-wire fence, staring down at Mark.

"Deactivate fence so we can retrieve the intruder," the voice boomed again.

There was a buzzing, and then Trey saw one of the men bend down and pull Mark's body under the fence. The barbed wire caught on his clothes, but the man didn't seem to care.

"Retrieval finished. Reactivate," the first man said. Trey saw that he was speaking into a walkie-talkie of sorts.

One of the other men lifted Mark and tossed him over his shoulder, carrying him like a sack of potatoes. Mark's eyelids fluttered—he was alive!

But then the lights went out. The men marched away, and Trey was left alone once again.

CHAPTER *SIXTEEN*

Trey didn't move for a long time. He couldn't. He was paralyzed. It was like he believed that if he stood there long enough, everything would reverse itself before his eyes: The light would come back on. The men would march backward and unload Mark onto the ground. Mark would crawl backward through the barbed wire, safe and sound, his clothes magically repaired, his body untouched by electricity.

Except Trey wanted the reversal to go further than that. He wanted Lee and Nina to be un-kidnapped, Mr. Talbot to be un-arrested, the Government to be unchanged. He wanted to be back at Hendricks—no, he wanted to be back at home.

He wanted his father to be alive.

Trey stopped there, in that cozy time when someone else made all his decisions for him, when someone else took care of him, when someone else told him what to do.

He had nobody now. Nobody and nothing.

Whimpering shamelessly, he wrapped his arms tightly across his chest. The papers he'd taken from the Grants' and the Talbots' rustled under his shirt. The fingers of his left hand brushed the top of his pants pocket and he reached on in and cradled his fake I.D. in his hand once again.

Okay, he had nothing except papers and a fake identity card. So what?

In the dimness of the woods, he staggered backward and almost tripped over the knapsack of food Mark had put down right before he climbed the fence. Even possessing food seemed pointless to Trey now. Bitterly, he kicked at the knapsack, and that actually felt good to him, as good as kicking a ball in a game back at Hendricks with Lee and the rest of his friends. He kicked the knapsack again, and it sailed so far away he didn't know where it landed.

He didn't go looking for it, just collapsed in a helpless heap on the ground.

Lee, I wanted to help you, he silently appealed to his friend—his friend he probably would never see again. *I tried.* But had he tried hard enough? *Mark did. Mark did everything he possibly could. And Mark—I'm sorry I can't save you, either.*

A familiar feeling seeped through Trey. Resignation. He felt the way he'd always felt playing chess with his father, back home. They'd be going along, Trey losing a few pieces, his father losing a piece or two—and then suddenly Trey would look at the board and realize he was trapped.

Nothing he could do would prevent his father from winning. And then his father would chuckle—how Trey hated that chuckle!—and say, "It's the endgame now."

Endgame. That's exactly where Trey was. The Population Police had Lee and Nina. They had Mark. They had the entire country lined up and ready to serve them. It was only a matter of time before they had Trey. Before they killed him.

Except . . .

Trey remembered a certain chess game he'd once played with his father. The very last one. He'd been moving his pieces around the board as usual, without much hope, agonizing over his father's every comment: "Are you sure you want to leave your bishop there?" . . . "Where do you think I'm going to move my rook next?" And then something had changed in the game. Trey moved a pawn and his father fell silent. He moved his queen and his father gritted his teeth.

And in the end, Trey won. He'd worked his way out of a trap he'd thought was inescapable. And he'd managed to set a trap of his own.

Was there any way he could still win now? Was there any way he could rescue Mark and Lee—and stay alive?

Not when I've got just a bunch of worthless papers and a fake I.D. It's not like that's going to help me get past those fences. There's no way in.

Except there was. The Population Police were letting hundreds of men and boys in through the front gates.

Trey got chills as an idea seized him. He almost wished his brain didn't work so well; he almost longed for the old paralysis of thinking there was nothing he could do. This was the most dangerous idea he'd ever had in his entire life.

But he was going to do it.

He, Trey—the biggest coward in the world, a third child who'd spent most of his life in hiding—was going to join the Population Police.

CHAPTER *SEVENTEEN*

T rey stood at the back of the line, his knees locked, his muscles trembling. It took every ounce of courage he had just to stand still, moving only every ten minutes or so—and even then, only inching forward, closer and closer to the fearsome gates.

He needed to plan, to plot out exactly what he was going to do once he got inside. Would he put on the Population Police uniform and ask to be a guard, then set Mark and Lee and the others free at his first opportunity? Or demand to see someone in charge, then pull the papers from his shirt like a magician: "Voilà! I have these secret documents from the homes of enemies of the state. If you don't release certain prisoners, I will set them on fire, and those secrets will be lost to the Population Police forever!"

He didn't have a match.

The papers weren't secret documents. They were financial forms, business incorporation papers, grocery lists. Nothing the Population Police would bargain for.

Nothing they couldn't grab from his hand, regardless.

What if I get to the front of the line before I have a plan? Trey's panicked brain asked him. *I should get out of line, think it all over, and come back when I know what I'm doing.*

But the line was hours long. He was already acutely aware of the seconds speeding by, the minutes melting away. Each passing moment made it more likely that Trey was already too late to help his friends.

Could he get help from any of the people standing near him? He looked around at rags and filth, shirts with patches on top of patches. He didn't have the nerve to look into anyone's face, let alone try to catch someone's eye.

They're joining the Population Police. What do I expect? I'm all alone in this.

And yet, he didn't quite feel alone. He kept hearing echoes in his mind: All the times Lee had said to him, "Come on, Trey! You can do it!" when he was trying to catch a football or hit a Wiffle ball, back at Hendricks School. All the times Mr. Hendricks had murmured, "You know, you really are an incredibly intelligent boy," when he sent Trey on errands. All the times his own father had nodded and smiled and said, "Yes, yes, that's right. You've learned this perfectly," when Trey recited his daily lessons, back home.

Trey kept shuffling forward, kept quelling his panic, kept trying to plan, kept listening to the encouraging echoes in his mind.

And then suddenly he found himself at the front of the line, before a phalanx of tables that blocked the entrance-way to the Grants' gates.

"I.D. card, please," a man growled.

Trey willed his hands not to shake as he reached into his pocket and pulled out the plastic card. He laid it on the table between him and the man.

"Travis Jackson," the man read in a bored voice.

Trey winced at the sound of the name that belonged to him, but wasn't his. He braced himself for the man to squint at the picture and compare it with Trey's face. And what if the man decided to test the I.D.? Trey had heard there were special chemicals, certain types of acids that would burn through a fake I.D. but leave an authentic one unscathed. They were expensive, so they weren't used often, but what if the Population Police chose to use them now, on Trey's card? Should he be braced to run, just in case?

But the man just tossed the I.D. to another man.

"Squad 3-C," the man announced, and the first man wrote something down on a pad of paper.

"Go on in," he said, lifting a hinged section of the table for Trey to pass through. "Report to the first room on the right, and they'll issue your uniform."

Trey hesitated.

"Don't I get my I.D. back?" he squeaked.

"You're part of the Population Police now, kid," the man said, chuckling. "You don't have any other identity any-more."

"But—" Trey knew better than to argue. He knew he shouldn't do anything that would fix his name or face in anyone's mind. He shouldn't do anything that would attract attention in any way. But how could he just walk away and leave that I.D.? It was the only thing his mother had left him with. What hope did he have without it?

The man didn't hear him.

"Next," he called, as the second man added Trey's I.D. to a huge stack in a box under the table.

Trey stood still, trying to decide whether to speak up again or not.

"Ya going to go in or get out of my way?" somebody snarled behind him. "'Cause I'm hungry. Haven't et in three days. I'm hoping they feed us first thing."

Trey swallowed hard.

"Go in," he said. Leaving his I.D. card behind, he stepped past the table and through the gates of the Grants' former estate.

The surge of other new Population Police recruits carried him along the driveway and up the stairs through the Grants' front door. Until he was past it, Trey didn't even think to look for the spot on the driveway where the huge chandelier had come crashing down, killing Mr. and Mrs. Grant and endangering Lee, before Trey rescued him.

I was brave here before, Trey told himself. *I can be brave again.*

He kept walking.

When the press of bodies around him finally parted,

Trey found himself inside a huge room he barely recognized. Surely he'd stood here before, the night of the Grants' fatal party, but the room looked totally different now. Trey remembered silks and satins and shimmering glass; now the room was filled with racks and racks of gray uniforms.

"Size?" a man asked Trey.

"Um, I don't know. I think I've grown since the last time I—"

"Never mind," the man said, thrusting a uniform into Trey's arms.

The fabric felt scratchy against Trey's skin. The Population Police emblem stared up at him from a sleeve of the uniform: two circles interlinked, with a teardrop shape beneath. Trey had heard all sorts of rumors about the meaning of the emblem. Some said the circles stood for two children, and the falling shape for the tears of mothers who had to kill their thirds. Others said the teardrop was actually a shovel, meant to bury the children the Population Police killed. Either way, being so close to the hated emblem made Trey's stomach seize up. He let the uniform drop to the ground and he doubled over, retching.

Suddenly someone slammed a fist into the side of his head.

"Boy!" a man screamed. "You treat that uniform with respect! You pick that up this instant! You hear?"

"Yes, sir," Trey managed to choke out. He scrambled to pick up the shirt and pants. The man was still screaming—

something about "pride in the organization you have just joined" and "our noble cause." Around him, Trey could feel the other recruits staring in shocked silence. Some had stopped in the middle of changing, standing half-naked, with only one arm or one leg shoved into the new uniforms.

Nobody came to Trey's defense.

"What do you have to say for yourself?" the man finished up.

"Please—I just—is there a bathroom somewhere?" Trey managed to stammer.

The man hit Trey again, knocking him against the wall. Trey tasted a trickle of blood in his mouth. He reached up and felt his face gingerly, but decided the blood came from a self-inflicted wound—he'd bit his tongue.

"Now finish up in here and report to the next room immediately!" the man yelled—not just at Trey this time, but at all the recruits.

"Yes, sir," some of them yelled, and the room became a flurry of activity again, as everyone crammed on the uniforms as quickly as possible.

Someone tapped Trey on the shoulder.

"Bathroom's over that way," a boy who was already fully dressed told him.

"Th-thank you," Trey said.

He crawled through the tangle of feet, no longer caring about humiliation or pain or even the need to rescue Mark and Lee. He just wanted to hide.

The bathroom, when he found it, was a vision in elegant silver wallpaper, obviously left over from the Grants. Trey shut the door tight and stared at his pale, terrified face in the mirror.

"What am I going to do?" he whispered to his reflection. Even his best ideas for bargaining or sneaking his friends out seemed like childish fantasies in the face of real fists and screams and all those gray uniforms.

Someone rattled the door handle outside.

"Hey! Give somebody else a turn!"

Trey peered frantically around the bathroom, as if hoping that the walls themselves might swallow him up, hide him for good. He couldn't face the world outside this room right now. He just couldn't.

But for all its elegance, the bathroom was fairly small and basic. It held a toilet and a sink. They were both stylized and sophisticated, but the sink didn't even have a cabinet underneath that Trey might have hidden in. And there wasn't a closet. Just a vent above the toilet, covered in a huge, fancy brass grille.

A vent. A covered vent.

His mind racing, Trey stared at the pattern in the brass grille. Hadn't he been wishing that the walls could swallow him up? Wasn't a vent essentially a hole in the wall?

Trey rushed toward the wall, tripping over his feet in his haste. He started to fall, but his knees hit the toilet, and he turned the fall into a faster way to climb toward the vent: He put the Population Police uniform on the back of the toilet and stood on the seat.

The grille probably has screws holding it in place, and I won't be able to take them off, he thought as he reached for the vent. But no—the grille was attached to the wall with a series of clasps and hinges that Trey figured out instantly. He unhooked the grille in a flash, and pulled it back from the wall.

I won't be able to fit, he thought. *My shoulders will be too broad. This is hopeless!*

But again, he was panicking for no reason.

He climbed up from the seat to the back of the toilet, and stuck his head and shoulders through the hole in the wall. It wasn't comfortable, and he had very little wiggle room. But he did fit.

Thinking hard, he backed out and then climbed in again, this time feet first.

I'll be too heavy. The air duct will collapse under my weight, he worried, but this fear didn't bother him much. As long as the duct didn't collapse loudly, and didn't fall too far, it would still be a safe place to hide.

He slid both feet in, then his torso and chest, and the duct showed no sign of giving way. At the last moment, he reached down and pulled the Population Police uniform in after him. He didn't think the Population Police officials had kept track of which uniform went to which recruit, but he didn't want to take any chances or leave any evidence behind.

What if I can't put the grille back on from the inside?

he wondered. But this fear too was needless. He pulled the grille down on its hinges and, by reaching back out through the holes, managed to reattach all but one of the clasps. Nobody would notice one out-of-place clasp, he assured himself.

Breathing hard, Trey scooted backward down the duct so nobody would be able to see his face at the grille.

Someone was rattling the doorknob again. This time, whoever it was started pounding on the door, too.

"Come out now!" a voice yelled. "This instant!"

This voice sounded more official. It might even have belonged to the officer who'd punched Trey before.

Trey held his breath.

Moments later, he heard a splintering sound. Through the narrow range of view the grille provided, he could see the bathroom door swing open.

"There's nobody in here!" the official-sounding voice cried out in disgust.

Then Trey heard a yelp of pain, which probably meant that the official was punching whoever had summoned him to the bathroom.

But nobody put his face up to the grille to look for Trey. Nobody seemed to notice he'd disappeared. Nobody called out, "Travis Jackson! Come out of hiding right now!"

Trey breathed a huge but silent sigh of relief.

He was safe.

He congratulated himself on his brilliance. *Mr. Hendricks is right*, he thought. *I am a genius.* He felt as triumphant as if he'd just single-handedly defeated the Population Police.

Maybe I can, he thought. And depending on where the duct led, he might have just discovered a way to save Mark and Lee and the others.

CHAPTER *EIGHTEEN*

T rey slid down the duct backward, dragging the Population Police uniform behind him. It was slow going, because he had so little room to maneuver, and because he was terrified of making any noise. More than once the buttons of his flannel shirt scraped against the metal duct, and then he froze, horrified at the thought that someone might be about to rip the duct apart, screaming out, "Aha! You! We know everything now! You're not Travis Jackson! You're about to die!"

No, they'll just think that the Grant house has mice, Trey comforted himself. *They'll put out poison, and I can avoid that.*

Trey knew he wasn't thinking very rationally. But he kept inching onward, feet first. That began to bother him. He wished he had eyes on his toes. What if he was about to kick out another brass grille? What if he were about to slide out into another room—one less innocuous than the bathroom? What if he was at this very moment slipping past some sort of opening that anyone could see? Trey kept turning his head and looking back over his shoulder, but that gave him a terrible crick in his neck, and he could barely see past his own body anyway. And there seemed to be nothing but darkness ahead.

He kept going.

When it seemed as though he had been crawling backward for hours, he hit a metal wall where he'd expected open air. Was he disoriented, crawling crooked? No—the wall extended on, straight and smooth, totally blocking his path. Had he reached a dead end? How could a duct just end like that? He didn't let himself panic. He stretched his legs out, tapping experimentally in all directions with his toes, and discovered that the metal walls he'd expected to find were missing to his left and right. Suddenly it all made sense: He'd reached a fork in his path, the place where the duct leading to the bathroom branched off from some main line. This was his route to the rest of the house.

"Right or left? Which will it be?" he muttered to himself. He tried to picture the ductwork in relationship to the floor plan of the entire house. He thought the left fork led toward the front door, and so was probably useless, but that was mostly just a guess. He moved his feet toward the right and began painstakingly turning the corner. Then he stopped, mid-turn.

"Stupid," he said under his breath. "Don't you know you can go face first now?"

He retreated, shoved his feet the opposite direction

down the duct, and soon was crawling forward, feeling his way with his hands and fingers instead of his feet and toes. He still couldn't see anything ahead of him, but the change made him feel better.

I ought to challenge Lee and the other boys to a heat duct race as soon as we get back to school, he thought. *I'd beat everyone.*

He was almost enjoying crawling through darkness.

Heroism by hiding, he thought. *Now, that I can handle. I'll have to change my motto. What would it be in Latin?*—Virtus, *I think, for "heroism," and* latente *for "hiding. . . ."*

That was when he saw the light.

At first it was just a gray shadow up ahead, a slight variation on all the endless blackness. But as he scurried forward, trying harder than ever to crawl silently, the brightness grew. Soon he could see a whole patterned grid of light in the duct in front of him. And he could hear voices.

"Unacceptable! Unacceptable, I tell you!" a man sputtered.

The voice sounded vaguely familiar, but at first Trey couldn't place it. It wasn't Mr. Talbot or Mr. Hendricks or any of his teachers at school. It wasn't the screaming man from the uniform room. What other men's voices had Trey ever heard?

Cautiously, he moved toward the light and peeked out a grille that was even larger and fancier than the one in the bathroom. He was looking down at a dark-haired man sitting at a huge desk. Rows of uniformed Population Police officers sat before him, like schoolchildren being scolded. Trey jerked back quickly, afraid one of them might look up at the wrong time. He rested his cheek against the cool metal of the duct, and listened to the pounding of his heart. What if they'd already seen him? What if they could hear his heartbeat too?

But nobody screamed out, "Hey! There's a boy hiding behind that grille!" Nobody yelled, "Capture him!" Gradually, Trey's terror ebbed, and he could listen again.

"We are in charge now!" the man continued his tirade. "*I* am in charge now!"

And suddenly Trey knew who the man was. Trey had heard his voice only once before, on television, at the Talbots' house. Trey was eavesdropping on Aldous Krakenaur, the head of the Population Police, and now, the head of the entire country.

And unless Aldous Krakenaur decided to send all his men away, letting Trey crawl on past, Trey was trapped there, a mere sneeze or a cough away from being discovered by his worst enemy.

CHAPTER *NINETEEN*

O f course, thinking about sneezing or coughing instantly made Trey want to do both. He thought about crawling backward, maybe even all the way to the bathroom where he'd started. But his fears about buttons rattling against the duct had multiplied tenfold. He didn't think he was physically capable of moving right now. He lay paralyzed, listening in terror.

"Don't you understand that we are everything now?" Krakenaur lectured. "I appropriated this house because it was the only building in the entire country suitable to the grandeur of my Government, the glory of my vision."

And because the Grants were dead and couldn't object, Trey thought. He wondered if any of the Population Police sitting so obediently before their leader knew the truth. He felt a little more daring just to be able to think defiant thoughts.

"So I arrive today, ready to rest and savor the accomplishments of my first few glorious days in office. And what do I discover? Ragamuffins trampling my front yard, tracking dirt into my glorious entry hall. Prisoners in the basement—where is the glory and dignity and vision in that? I want a headquarters worthy of my honor!" He seemed to be pounding his fist on the desk to punctuate that last sentence.

There was a shocked silence, as if none of the officers knew how to respond. Trey felt equally stunned.

Prisoners in the basement . . . prisoners in the base- ment . . . Had Krakenaur just told Trey exactly where to find his friends? What other prisoners could there be?

Now the officers were mumbling among themselves.

"*You* issued the order to take new recruits," someone said resentfully.

"But surely there's a back entrance?" Krakenaur spat out. "Or some hut nearby that we could appropriate for processing purposes?"

Nobody answered. Trey wondered if the officers were nodding obediently or looking dubious.

"And it's not like there are hundreds of prisoners in the basement," someone else muttered. "There's just one."

One? Trey's heart sank. Then it was probably just Mark down there. Where could Lee and the others be?

Another officer was adding in a soothing voice, "Anyhow, we're just keeping that prisoner here until we finish our interrogation. Then we'll dispose of him. It won't be more than a few more hours."

Trey gulped so hard he feared the entire roomful of men

could hear him. *A few more hours . . .* Trey didn't have time to wait for Krakenaur to finish browbeating his officers and dismiss them all. He would have to crawl past them and go rescue Mark *now.*

Trey stared at the pattern of light coming in through the fancy grille as though he could will it into darkness. Wait a minute—maybe he could. It probably looked dark to the people outside right now. He just had to make sure they didn't see a changing pattern of skin, hair, flannel shirt, dark pants. . . . Carefully, he spread out the shirt of the Population Police uniform on the bottom of the duct. Then, very quickly—so quickly he didn't have time to think about the danger—he lifted the shirt so it covered the entire grille from the inside.

Nobody noticed.

Trey gave himself a few moments to take deep breaths of relief. Then he slipped forward, holding the shirt in place over the grille with his hands, then his torso, then his legs.

He didn't worry about rattling buttons once.

The entire procedure was going so smoothly, Trey was starting to think he had a future as a contortionist. And then, just as he was moving his leg away from the grille, he glanced back and realized: The uniform shirt had caught on his belt as he'd slid past. He'd been in full view of anyone who cared to look for the past two minutes.

Instantly, he jerked his leg away from the grille, only barely managing to stop himself from kicking the other side of the duct with a solid thump. And then he waited.

Did anybody see me?

It was torture, waiting, knowing he could do nothing now to correct his mistake. But down below, Krakenaur just kept berating his men.

"We have a duty to our people!" he was yelling.

Nobody had been looking at the grille. Nobody had seen Trey.

Oh, thank you, he thought, feeling as if every moment for the rest of his life would be a pure gift. Because it was. He'd deserved to be discovered, and he hadn't been.

He turned his attention to finding Mark.

Over the next hour or so, Trey despaired repeatedly of ever finding a way down to the basement. The ducts of the Grant mansion were like a maze, twisting and turning and branching off at odd intervals. More than once, Trey considered just turning around, climbing out a vent in some empty room, and then looking for actual stairs down to the basement. But seeing Krakenaur had chilled him. Trey could practically feel the danger in every room of the house—everywhere outside the ducts. He wore a hole in the knee of his pants, crawling; he rubbed the palms of his hands raw from feeling his way along. But that was still better than being out in the midst of the Population Police.

And then, finally, as Trey reached a tired arm out yet again into the endless darkness, he touched—nothing. Just a hole where the duct plunged straight down.

Trey hadn't thought about its working that way. He'd been thinking of a nice gentle slope—something like the slides he'd seen in pictures of playgrounds.

I can do this, Trey told himself. *I have to.*

He reached across the hole, feeling around for the wall on the other side. As soon as he touched metal, he pulled his upper body over the hole and thrust his legs down it, bracing his feet and knees along the side of the metal chute. He banged his head on the top of the duct, and his leg muscles began trembling with the strain almost immediately. But he didn't fall. He inched down, each move absolute agony.

How much farther can it possibly be? Trey wondered. *How high are the Grants' ceilings?*

Finally, Trey's foot brushed something directly below him. He straightened out his legs, delighted that he'd soon be standing on solid ground.

Well, solid duct, anyway, he corrected himself.

He eased his stiff, aching arms away from the walls of the duct so all his weight was on his legs and the duct below.

Suddenly there was a ripping sound. Trey plunged straight down. As he reached out frantically, clutching for anything that might stop his fall, his fingers brushed plastic. He grabbed what seemed to be a plastic tube, which swung down to the right. Seconds later, he hit a concrete floor with a muffled thud.

Trey lay still, too stunned even to try out his arms and

legs and make sure that nothing was broken. In near-darkness, he peered straight up, trying to comprehend what had happened. He'd broken through the duct, of course, but why? He looked at the plastic tube he still hugged to his chest. Oh. He was in the basement, and the ducts down here were evidently plastic, not metal. The tube he was clutching was about as flimsy as a garbage bag.

At least it was strong enough to break your fall, he told himself reassuringly. *And nobody knows I'm here.*

"What was that?" someone yelled.

Correction, Trey thought. *At least they haven't found me yet. At least I have time to hide.*

He glanced around, but he was in an empty room.

I'll hide in the tube, then, he told himself. But the plastic duct was too narrow. Even if he managed to climb into it in time, his shoulders would cause the tube to bulge. He'd be discovered instantly if anyone came to investigate.

Then it's back into the metal duct, Trey thought, still feeling amazingly calm.

He stood—his legs did still work, after all—and reached up.

The bottom of the metal duct was a good two feet above his fingertips. He had nothing to stand on, he couldn't jump that high—there was no way out.

And he could hear footsteps coming his way.

CHAPTER *TWENTY*

Know what I think that noise was?" a second voice called out. "Mice. Or rats, maybe. Hey, tell you what. You run back there and flush them out, drive them straight toward my cage, and I'll catch them with my bare hands. I've done it before. Ever had rat roasted on an open flame? Mmm-mmm. Delicious."

It was Mark's voice, sounding twangier and more hickish than ever. Trey's knees went weak with relief.

But so what? Trey reminded himself. *That just means the two of us will be imprisoned together.*

The footsteps stopped.

"I am a master guard in the Population Police," the first voice snapped. "I don't eat rats."

"Hey, hey, didn't mean to insult you," Mark said. "I should have thought about who I was talking to. I ain't used to being around fancy officials and all. It probably ain't rats or mice, nohow. Not here. Not some highfalutin place like this."

"Hmmph," the guard said. But, miraculously, he didn't continue walking toward Trey's room. Instead, he muttered, "No funny business." And then his footsteps began to retreat. Trey thought, by the way they echoed, that he might even be climbing stairs.

Trey exhaled very slowly. He took another deep breath, then tiptoed to a doorway that seemed to lead out into the rest of the basement. Feeling ridiculously brave, he peeked around the corner.

Mark was, indeed, crouched inside a cage, out in the middle of the floor. The cage was small—Mark couldn't have stood up in it. Trey had the impression that the cage wasn't even meant for humans. It was like the Population Police were just improvising, using whatever they could find lying around at the Grants'.

Will that make it easier for me to set him free? Trey wondered.

The guard wasn't anywhere in sight now, but Mark's cage was directly under a large, glaring overhead light. *I'll wait until they turn that out,* Trey thought. *Then I'll creep nearby.* A pile of boxes stood behind the cage. Trey could hide there.

Trey's plans were shaping up nicely. The only problem was, what were he and Mark going to do after Trey released him? If they had time to slide a stack of boxes over under the broken metal duct . . . if they could do it quietly . . . if the boxes were sturdy enough to climb on . . . if they were able to climb back up the duct . . . if everything fell into place, he and Mark would be safe.

Trey didn't like dealing with so many ifs, but he didn't think he had a choice. He sat back, waiting until the light went out.

Instead, after just a few minutes, the guard called down, "Prisoner, prepare to be interrogated."

Trey grimaced, remembering the conversation he'd overheard earlier. *We're just keeping that prisoner here until we finish our interrogation. Then we'll dispose of him. It won't be more than a few more hours.* What if he didn't have time to rescue Mark before they took him away? How much time had Trey already lost wandering around in the heat ducts?

Trey glanced around the corner into the next room once more. And then, before he had time to reconsider, he dashed out and slipped between the pile of boxes and the wall.

Trey ran as silently as possible, but Mark saw him. And positively beamed.

Then he had to erase the smile from his face. Footsteps were coming down the stairs toward them. Trey ducked behind the boxes. A small gap between them gave him a narrow view of Mark's cage. Trey saw a Population Police officer striding toward Mark. The chest of the officer's uniform was completely covered with medals. Trey had a feeling that this guy ranked a lot higher than the guard.

"Explain why you were trying to sneak into our headquarters," the officer snapped at Mark.

"We-ell, see, I didn't actually know it was your head-quarters," Mark said, drawing out his words to make himself sound slow and stupid. "And I weren't trying to sneak in."

Mark sounded so dumb and innocent, Trey had to smile. Who would have guessed Mark would be such a great actor?

"I was just out in the woods looking for food when I seen the fence," Mark continued. "I didn't know nothing about this place 'cept it belonged to somebody rich. Wouldn't have even come near the fence, 'cepting that this squirrel, see, he run right under the barbed wire. And I was chasing him so hard, I didn't never think about it being a problem, me stepping past that fence. I wasn't hurting nothing. And then—zap! That's the last thing I remember until I woke up here. So how about it? How about setting me free so I can go get that squirrel?"

The Population Police officer snorted.

"Hunting is a violation of numerous governmental codes. Do you realize you've just confessed to a serious crime?"

Mark hung his head.

"Yes, sir," he said. "Now I do. But it weren't like I had a gun or nothing—just a bow and arrow. And I was awful hungry."

"Didn't you know the Population Police offered food to anyone who joined up—them and their families?" the officer asked.

"No, sir," Mark said. "Ain't never heard that. Can I still

do it? Where do I go to join up? I'd be a good employee. And it'd just be me you'd have to feed—my mam and pap passed on near about five year ago, and I ain't got no brother or sister or other kin at all."

The officer regarded Mark in silence. Then he asked, "What happened to your bow and arrow?"

Mark blinked at him.

"Well, shoot," he said. "I don't know. Reckon I must have dropped it when that fence zapped me." His face brightened. "Hey, I know. You go find my bow and arrow. Then you'll know I'm telling the truth."

The officer narrowed his eyes, as if suspecting a trap. Then he seemed to decide that Mark wasn't smart enough to try a trap.

"*I'm* not about to go traipsing out there in the woods looking for your illegal weapons," the officer said indignantly. "But—I'll send one of my men after it. Then maybe we'll just see what to do about you."

And he turned on his heel and walked away.

Trey stayed hidden until he was sure the officer had climbed the stairs again. Then he poked his head out.

"Wow, Mark, how'd you know he'd fall for that?" Trey whispered.

"It was written all over his face, that he was dying to go order someone around. And that he thought I was dumber than pond slime. I thought about what you'd said about grammar, and I turned it around—I was saying 'ain't' on purpose, you know."

"I know," Trey said.

"So I bought us some time, but I don't know how much. I can always say somebody must have stolen the bow and arrow if he comes back soon. But I hope it don't come to that—how about getting me out of here now?"

"Okay, okay," Trey muttered. He slipped out from behind the boxes. Squinting in the glare—and terrified of being so exposed—Trey felt around for some sort of latch to release the door of the cage.

But the cage didn't have a latch. It was fastened with a thick lock.

"Mark—I'd need a key—," Trey sputtered.

"No you don't," Mark said soothingly. "Just some pliers or wire cutters—even a piece of bent wire to pick the lock."

"Where am I supposed to get that?" Trey asked.

"This is a basement, isn't it? Look around!"

Trey retreated to his boxes, figuring he could at least stay partially hidden while he looked there. The first box held table linens. The one beside it held china wrapped in layers and layers of thin crinkly paper.

"Trey?" Mark whispered. "Thanks for coming to get me. I never in a million years thought you'd be so brave. I thought I was on my own."

"I haven't saved you yet," Trey said through gritted teeth. He was on the third box, which held more table-cloths.

"How'd you get down here?" Mark asked.

MARGARET PETERSON HADDIX

Quickly, talking as he searched, Trey told him. Mark gave a soft, admiring whistle.

"You joined the Population Police?" he asked. "You crawled through heat ducts past *Aldous Krakenaur*? I had you figured all wrong. You're the bravest kid I know!"

Trey didn't have time to get puffed up with pride. He was on the last box in the stack. This one was full of fancy crystal vases.

Panic-stricken, he looked around. Were there boxes in some other part of the basement? Wouldn't the Grants have had *something* useful down here?

But the boxes and Mark's cage were the only things in the entire basement.

Trey fought to hide his fear from Mark. He tugged on the lock as if he thought he could break it with his bare hands. Mark saw.

"Oh," Mark said, and turned his face away.

"Maybe—," Trey said, but he didn't have a plan to suggest.

Just then they heard footsteps on the stairs again. Trey dove behind the boxes once more, just before the Population Police official burst around the corner.

"You were not hungry," the official snarled at Mark. "How do you explain this?"

He held something out to Mark. Trey couldn't tell what it was at first, but when he shifted his position and saw what was dangling from the official's hand, it was all he could do not to gasp.

The official was holding the knapsack Mark had carried from the truck. It was the knapsack Mark had put down right before he'd tried to crawl through the barbed-wire fence, the knapsack Trey had kicked away in disgust.

The knapsack full of food.

"What do you mean, 'How do you explain this?'" Mark asked. "I've never seen that before in my life. What is it?"

But his voice shook, and he'd waited a second too long in answering. It was all too clear that he *had* seen that knapsack before. That it belonged to him.

The official slowly loosened the knapsack's strings and began pulling out its contents. A box of raisins. A bag of peanuts. An apple. Two apples. Three. Potatoes. Bananas. Peaches. Cereal.

"I'll ask you again," the official said. "Why were you trying to sneak into Population Police headquarters?"

"I wasn't," Mark said. But his voice was even weaker now. The most gullible fool in the world wouldn't have believed him.

"You were," the official said calmly. He seemed to be relishing his role. "And now I will pronounce your sentence. You will be executed at dawn."

Mark gasped. Trey reeled backward, hitting the wall. He barely managed to avoid crying out in pain. This was all his fault. Why had he kicked that knapsack and then just left it behind? Why hadn't he taken it with him, or hidden it somewhere safe?

Even bravery's not enough when you make stupid

mistakes, Trey thought. It was ironic—yes, now he truly understood that word. Trey had always prided himself on his brilliance and been ashamed of his cowardice. But now that he'd actually shown a little courage, his idiocy had condemned his friend to death.

All I'm really good for is remembering foreign languages, and they're useless, Trey thought. But then he had a flash of memory: When he'd been crouching in terror on the Talbots' front porch, his knowledge of Latin had actually seemed to be the thing that saved his life. Why? What was so special about translating *"liber"* into "free"?

For the first time, Trey thought maybe he understood. What if *"liber"* and "free" were code words—code words for people who believed in more freedom than the Population Police allowed?

Trey waited until the official had walked away, and then he whispered to Mark, "I think I know how to save you. Yell, *'liber!'"*

"Huh?" Mark said.

"Liber," Trey said. "It means 'free.'"

"Liber!" Mark yelled.

"Do it again," Trey whispered. "And again. And throw some 'Free's' in there too."

"Liber!" Mark repeated obediently. *"Liber! Liber!* Free! *Liber!* Free! *Liber!* Free!"

At first, he was just saying the words. But soon his voice took on a plaintive strain, as if he were truly begging for freedom. It gave Trey chills. He hoped the sound would seep through the broken duct and out the fancy grilles into Aldous Krakenaur's office.

Mark yelled until he was hoarse. But the only thing that happened was that the guard turned the light out, and Mark fell silent.

CHAPTER *TWENTY-ONE*

Mark?" Trey whispered. "It's all my fault. I left the knapsack out there. I kicked it away, and then I forgot about it."

"I forgot about it too," Mark whispered back in a husky voice.

"They gave me a uniform. Maybe if I put it on and pretend to be a guard, I could—oh, no," Trey groaned.

"What?" Mark said.

"I left the uniform back in the heat duct on the first floor," Trey confessed. He hadn't pulled it along with him when he'd shimmied down the duct to the basement. He hadn't even thought about the uniform then.

"Oh," Mark said. That one short word, a mere syllable, spoke volumes. Mark had given up. "You—you should probably go now," Mark added. "So they don't catch you, too."

"No," Trey said, finally sitting down, rather than crouching, behind the boxes. "Nobody's looking for me, and you got the guard scared of mice and rats. I'll stay until——as long as I can."

He wasn't about to say, "until they execute you." Still, the unspoken words seemed to hang between them. After a few moments, Mark whispered, "Thanks."

For all the bad things that had happened in Trey's life, this was the first time that he'd known about a tragedy beforehand. His father dying, his mother abandoning him, the chauffeur leaving him behind, the Population Police taking over the Government—all of those calamities had been sudden and unexpected. It didn't seem fair to know that Mark was about to die, and not be able to stop it.

"Mark, what if you bend back the bars of the cage?" Trey asked. "You're strong—"

"I already tried," Mark said. "The cage is stronger." He was quiet for a minute, then said, "I think I understand better now how Luke always felt. It was like he was in a cage his whole life. And I just thought he was wimpy."

This was no time to remind Mark that it was dangerous to call Luke by his real name, that the fake name, Lee, was safer.

"And then he came back, and it was almost like he'd grown past me," Mark said, sounding as if he was in a daze. "He'd had adventures and he'd seen the world, and you know, that Peter kid—Smits—he treated Luke like he was the biggest hero ever." Mark hesitated, then went on. "I think I was jealous," he confessed.

Trey didn't think Lee had seen anything of the world

besides Hendricks School and the Talbot house, but he knew what Mark meant. Trey had always felt the same way about Lee. Back at Hendricks, Lee had even stood up to the traitor, Jason. And he'd run back into a burning building to save other boys. Trey had never understood where Lee got his courage. But—he thought of Mark as strong and brave as well.

"Mark, you came here trying to rescue your brother. You're a hero too," Trey argued.

"I didn't succeed," Mark whispered. "I don't even know where Luke is. And they're going to kill me, and my parents will never know what happened to either of us. Or—or maybe—maybe because of me, they'll track down Mother and Dad and Matthew and punish them, too. . . ." His voice cracked.

"Everything's a mess," Trey said. "But it's not your fault."

He didn't even know how he was going to manage to escape after Mark was gone. But it seemed selfish to think about his own future when Mark didn't have one.

"It was stupid to come here, to think I could help Luke," Mark said bitterly.

"No it wasn't," Trey argued. "We had to try."

His words sounded false to his own ears. Whatever danger Trey was in, he wasn't sitting in a cage, condemned to death, like Mark was. Who was Trey to tell Mark they'd done the right thing?

But Mark didn't seem mad at him.

"Trey?" Mark said. "If it'd been you in here and me out-side—I wouldn't have been brave enough to do what you did. I wouldn't have thought of joining the Population Police. And crawling through those ducts? A small space like that? I couldn't have done it. You're braver than me."

"People are brave in different ways," Trey said. The idea had just occurred to him.

"But—why did you do it?" Mark said. "No offense, but before I thought you were the most chicken kid I've ever met. Why did you come into Population Police headquar-ters looking for me?"

Trey pondered Mark's questions.

"I'm not sure," he finally answered. "Maybe I just didn't want to be left alone."

Mark choked back a laugh.

"There are a whole lot of easier ways to avoid being lonely," he said.

"I don't know," Trey said. "People are always leaving me behind. My dad died, my mother abandoned me, the chauffeur drove off without me. . . . You were the first per-son who didn't leave me behind on purpose. The first person who was planning to come back. So I had to do everything to find you."

Mark seemed to be absorbing this. Then he said, "Wait a minute. If your father died—well, it's not like he died on purpose, right?"

"I guess not," Trey said. He knew he couldn't really blame his dad for having a heart attack and dying. But he wasn't willing to let his dad off the hook so easily. He didn't want Mark thinking Trey's father had been some great guy who'd just died too soon.

"Listen to this, though," Trey said, the anger he'd been holding down for a year suddenly boiling over. "My dad got a fake I.D. for me way back when I was still a baby. But he kept me hidden, he didn't let me go anywhere—he didn't even tell me I *had* that I.D. Ever."

"Maybe your dad didn't think the I.D. was good enough. Like it was only an emergency backup. Just in case," Mark said.

"But then my mom, after my dad died, she just drove me to Hendricks School and dumped me out. Said it wasn't safe for me to see her ever again."

"That's what everyone said about Luke, too, when he left," Mark said.

"But which one of my parents was right?" Trey whispered.

"I don't know," Mark said. "What would you do if you had a third child?"

Trey had never asked himself this question. He'd never thought about what it would be like to be the one in control, with power over somebody else's fate. He remembered all the attention his father had given him, the way he'd always raved, "Your older brothers never cared for Latin. I'm so glad I have you!" And Trey, who'd never met his older brothers because they were much, much older and lived far, far away, had just glowed.

But he also remembered the strained look on his mother's face the day she left him behind at Hendricks. She'd been crying as she left.

Was it possible his parents both thought they were doing the right thing?

He and Mark had thought they were doing the right thing too, driving off in search of Lee. But Mark's parents probably didn't think so, now that they had two sons missing.

It was all too confusing, all the choices out in the world. All the mistakes that were possible.

No wonder Trey's dad had thought he was doing Trey a favor keeping him at home, teaching him grammar rules that made the world seem safe and orderly.

Trey closed his eyes briefly, as if that could ward off the confusion and the darkness. When he opened them again, he could see a dim light bobbing at the opposite side of the basement. A flashlight.

"Is it—is it dawn already?" Mark moaned. "Are they coming for me?"

"Shh," the person behind the flashlight hissed.

If some Population Police officers or guards were coming to take Mark away, why would they be concerned about silence? Why wouldn't they just turn on the light? What was going on?

CHAPTER *TWENTY-TWO*

The light drew nearer.

"Whisper," a voice instructed Mark. "Why were you yelling, '*liber*'?"

"I thought it might save my life," Mark said in a hushed tone. "Will it?"

The guard—for it was a guard; a different one, but still in a Population Police uniform—shone the light into Mark's face.

"How can a word save your life?" the guard asked.

"I don't know," Mark admitted.

Trey's heart sank. He hadn't explained. Mark didn't know. But then, it wasn't like Trey understood much either. He'd just been making guesses in the dark.

"Why that word?" the guard continued. "How did you know the word '*liber*'?

"A friend told me," Mark said.

"Who is this friend?"

"I can't tell you."

"Didn't this friend tell you to whisper, not to yell?"

"No," Mark said. "He told me to yell."

The guard kept his light trained on Mark's face. He seemed to be studying Mark very carefully.

"You are not one of us," the guard finally said. "You are a threat, not an ally. I cannot help you."

"Please—," Mark said.

But the guard was already walking away, his flashlight directed back toward the stairs.

"I'm begging you—" Mark pleaded.

The guard turned around.

"Perhaps your friend is a threat to us too. Perhaps you could tell us his name," he said.

Trey winced. The guard was bargaining now—bargaining for Trey's life as well as Mark's. What would Mark do?

"Why should I care about you?" Mark argued. "Remember? I'm not 'one of us.'"

The guard shrugged.

"Suit yourself," he said, and kept walking toward the stairs.

The sound of his footsteps pounded in Trey's ears like a cadence of doom. Each step made it less likely that Mark could be saved.

At what point would it become impossible?

Trey listened in agony. Then, just as the guard reached the bottom of the stairs, he could contain himself no longer.

"How can you use '*liber*' as a password if you don't

really believe in freedom?" Trey shouted. "How can you just stand by and let an innocent boy die?"

The guard turned around instantly and scanned the entire basement with his flashlight.

"Where are you?"

For the first time, Trey heard uncertainty in the guard's voice—maybe even fear.

"You don't know where I am," Trey taunted.

The beam of light came to rest on the pile of boxes Trey was crouched behind.

"You don't know how big he is," Mark added. "You don't know how many people are down here. And they're all on my side."

Trey was silently cheering Mark on, grinning over the bravado in Mark's voice. Mark sounded so confident, Trey almost felt like looking around for compatriots. Too late, the fear struck: What would Trey do if the guard stalked up the stairs and came back with a horde of Population Police officers?

But the guard didn't do that. He didn't move at all.

"Shh," he said. "What do you want?"

"To be free," Trey answered, before Mark could.

"You think yelling about it in the basement of the Population Police headquarters will do any good?" the guard asked.

"It got you down here, didn't it?" Mark asked.

The guard swept his beam of light all along the boxes. Was it just Trey's imagination, or did the guard let the light linger longest on the exact spot where Trey was hiding?

"If you've got a whole legion of friends down here with you, why do you need me?" the guard countered.

Mark didn't answer, and Trey was afraid to.

"Why did you come here?" the guard asked. "You and your friend?"

"We were looking for my brother," Mark said.

Trey inhaled sharply. If he'd been Mark, he wouldn't have answered that question.

"Is your brother a new recruit?" the guard asked.

"No," Mark said. "He was here before the Population Police took over. Do you know what might have happened to him?"

Now Trey was dizzy with fear. Maybe he was hyperventilating. He wanted to shout out to Mark, "Don't tell him anything else! You might get Lee killed!" But he couldn't speak.

Then the guard did something incredible. He sat down on the bottom step of the stairs.

"I, too, am worried about someone," he said softly. "Perhaps . . ."

"Perhaps what?" Mark asked.

The guard shook his head.

"I can't trust you," he said.

"I'm about to be killed," Mark said. "Don't you think I'd do just about anything to stay alive?"

The guard gave a little, amused snort, as if Mark had told a joke.

"That's not what I need. I need someone who'd hold on to principle and loyalty, even if it meant death," he said. "Not that it matters. I need lots of impossible things. Access to secret records. Fake documents. A car."

"I have a car," Mark said. "A truck, anyway."

The guard snorted again, this time in disbelief.

"You're in a cage," he said.

Trey strained to hear over the ringing in his ears. He was definitely hyperventilating. He fought against the urge to black out. He needed to think—and to think clearly. All he could hear were the guard's words, echoing in his mind again and again: *You're in a cage. . . . You're in a cage. . . .*

"*I'm* not," he whispered.

He stumbled out from behind the boxes. Act before thinking—that seemed to be his new motto. *Ante cogitatum, factum.* He stood on wobbly legs, but managed to keep his voice steady.

"*I'm* not in a cage," he said aloud, and waited for the guard's beam of light to find him.

CHAPTER *TWENTY-THREE*

They worked out a deal, Mark and Trey and the Population Police guard. Their negotiations seemed to take hours, because all of them were afraid of saying too much.

"How is it that you have a truck?" the guard asked. "And where is it?"

"We can't tell you," Mark said.

"Who are you worried about?" Trey asked.

"I will name no names," the guard said. "It is better for you not to know."

"What's your name?" Mark asked.

"It doesn't matter," the guard said. Trey tried to sneak covert glances at him, to get a good look at his face, but he stayed carefully in the shadows, the flashlight trained away from his features. And he didn't have a badge number or other identification on his uniform.

Could Mark and Trey trust him?

They didn't have much choice.

MARGARET PETERSON HADDIX

Trey had to give up one huge, valuable tidbit of information: He told the guard that it was possible to go between rooms at the Grants' house by crawling through the heat ducts. The guard nodded soberly at this news.

"So I can get access to the secret records," he mumbled. "And I can find the documents I want to fake. . . ."

"I'll do it," Trey said. "Tell me where to go and I'll get whatever you want. And then you'll set Mark free."

"No," the guard said. "Somebody else will do that job."

"Who?" Trey asked.

"Never mind," the guard said.

Trey was secretly relieved not to have to crawl through the ducts again. But his relief died when he realized what he'd have to do instead: drive the truck.

"My partner and I will have to confer," Trey announced when the three of them had finished all the planning.

"Fine," the guard said.

He walked to the other side of the room, but kept his flashlight trained on Mark and Trey.

"Mark, I can't!" Trey protested as quietly as possible. "Can't we ask him to put me in the cage and just have you drive?"

Mark looked across the room to where the guard sat, grim-faced.

"He doesn't trust us as it is," Mark said. "He'll think we're trying to trick him. Or that we're just bluffing. Besides, it's easy to drive. Just remember to push the clutch in when you're changing gears. And, oh yeah, you'll be driving forward most of the time, so you look out the front window, not the back. . . ."

"I need a decision," the guard said from across the room.

"We'll do it," Mark said.

And so it was that ten minutes later, Trey was climbing the stairs out of the basement. He'd changed into a fresh Population Police uniform the guard had given him, transferred his papers between pockets, and then stuffed his original clothes into one of the Grants' boxes. But this uniform wasn't the dull gray of a new recruit's. It was the more ominous-looking black of a prison guard's.

"I'll show you to the door," the guard said, escorting Trey down a dark hall. Other guards stood outside many of the rooms they passed, but they only glanced at Trey and his mysterious guide.

The entryway was empty now, the earlier crowd of recruits gone who-knew-where.

"It's four in the morning," the guard whispered as they stood on the doorstep. "If you're not back by six. . . ."

He didn't have to finish his sentence. If Trey wasn't back by six, Mark would die.

"I won't take long," Trey promised.

The guard handed him a clutch of official-looking papers.

"Authorizations," he said. "Show these at the servants' entrance when you return. Over there." He pointed vaguely, but Trey didn't ask for specifics. Finding the servants' entrance was the least of his worries.

He stepped out into the chilly night air, and the guard shut the door behind him.

Down the stairs, out the walkway, across the driveway. . . . Trey moved numbly, his fear of the outdoors trumped by greater fears. At the front gate, a sentry merely grunted at him. Outside the gate, men and boys were still lined up, but they were no longer standing. Most of them appeared to be sleeping, either slumped over or lying down on the hard ground. In the dark, all those motionless bodies made Trey think of pictures he'd seen of battlegrounds, after the battle was over.

"Hey! No cutting in line!" someone growled at him. A few large bodies shifted menacingly, blocking Trey's path. Not everyone was asleep after all.

"I—I'm not cutting in line," Trey stammered. "I'm—I'm already in the Population Police. See?"

He held out the insignia on his uniform, even though it was too dark to make out the circles and the teardrop.

Somebody grabbed Trey's sleeve, verifying by touch what couldn't be verified by sight.

"He's telling the truth," a voice announced, and miraculously, the path cleared ahead of Trey.

"Hey, man, did they feed you good?" another voice called out plaintively.

"Yes," Trey said, though it was a lie, of course. He'd eaten nothing since he and Mark had left the truck, all those hours ago. His stomach felt squeezed together, turned inside out. "They'll feed you when you get inside too," he added.

"When's that going to be?" someone grumbled. But Trey just kept walking, and nobody challenged him. Soon he'd left the long line of desperate men behind.

He and Mark had discussed the best route back to the truck.

"It'll take too long walking along the river," Mark had said. "There are streets you can take through the city. I remember from the map. I—I was just too scared to go that way before."

Oh, yeah, Trey thought now. *It's going to be much less scary at four in the morning. With me alone instead of following Mark.*

At first, though, his worries seemed unnecessary. The street leading away from the Grants' house was absolutely deserted. The streetlights weren't on, but Trey could see well enough in the dim glow from the moon. He didn't mind the darkness anyhow. It made it easier for him to believe that he was unseen, gliding through the shadows.

After a mile or two, he turned onto another street that made him remember the first bit of news he'd heard from Mrs. Talbot, about the riots. This street was full of stores that might once have been expensive boutiques. But every plate glass window had been smashed in. Some were now boarded up; others were just gaping open, their shelves picked clean.

Looters, Trey thought with a shiver, and began walking even faster.

After five blocks, Trey heard footsteps approaching. He

froze, looking for a place to hide, already worrying that he'd be too late to save Mark if he had to hide for very long. But the glow of a flashlight caught him before he had the chance to move.

"Identify yourself!" a voice called out.

Two men were approaching him. Trey's heart sank when he saw they were in Population Police uniforms. He didn't have his I.D. with him. It was still back at the Grants' house, in the stack with the other new recruits'.

"Don't be silly, Henrik," the second man said. "Can't you see he's Poppo? *And* he outranks us."

"Oh, sorry," the first man said, sounding humbled. "Where are you going, sir?"

Just from the voices, Trey guessed that both men were at least a decade older than him. But he decided to take a chance.

"My destination is classified information," he growled—figuring that growling would do more to lower his voice than anything else. His uniform had come with a cap, and he made sure it was pulled down, covering most of his face, so they couldn't see that he wasn't even old enough to shave. "And what's with this 'Poppo' business? That's disrespectful. You're proud members of the Population Police, and don't you forget it."

"Yes, sir," the two said in unison.

"What's your assignment?" Trey asked.

"We're patrolling," the first man said. "Enforcing cur-few."

"Then get busy," Trey commanded. "I thought I heard noises back there!" He pointed in the opposite direction.

"Yes, sir!" the men said, and rushed off.

Trey had to hold back a giggle as he watched them scurry away. He'd outsmarted and outbluffed the Population Police. Just because he was wearing a uniform. Just because they thought he outranked them.

Now I know what the soldiers in the Trojan horse felt like, he thought. *If I were living hundreds of years ago, people would write epic poems in my honor too. Something about "The third child in his enemy's clothes. . . ."*

He walked on, practically strutting, working out rhyme schemes in his head. Epic poems were always best in French. *Let's see. "Le troisième enfant dans les vêtements de ses ennemis . . ."*

He was so absorbed, he didn't hear the whispering until he was already surrounded.

CHAPTER TWENTY-FOUR

He's all by himself. . . ."

"Maybe he's carrying food. . . ."

"Maybe *his* food's not rotten. . . ."

"Who's there?" Trey called out, in a panic. "I said, who's there?"

He glanced around frantically, but he could see nothing but vacant storefronts and dark, impenetrable shadows. The tattered remains of a window-display dress blew in an unseen breeze, and Trey stiffened. But it was hanging from a mannequin, not a real live human.

"There are lots of Population Police patrolling in this area!" Trey cried out, even though he'd seen only the two men. "Watch out!"

"Maybe he has food. . . ."

"Food . . ."

"Food . . ."

The word echoed down the empty street. And then, in the blink of an eye, a mob of creatures rushed at Trey from all sides. At first, he almost thought they were animals, not humans—how big did feral cats get? But then they all began screaming at him at once.

"Where is it?"

"Give us your food!"

"Wait!" Trey protested. "I'm not—" But did he really want to announce that he wasn't truly a Population Police member? He got one glimpse of glittering eyes in an emaciated face—a woman's, he thought—and realized that these people wouldn't care if he was a third, fourth, or fifteenth child. They just wanted food.

He changed tactics.

"Listen!" he tried to explain. "I don't have any food with me. But if you join up, the Population Police will feed you and your family. . . ."

Somebody punched him.

"The Population Police's food was rotten!"

"It had weevils!"

"A dog couldn't eat that!"

"And now I won't see my little Johnny for three years!" the glittering-eyed woman finished up.

Trey was still reeling from the punch.

"I just—I'm not in charge of the food," he said. "I've got nothing to do with that."

The mob was closing in on him. They didn't even seem to hear his arguments. They didn't care.

Great, Trey thought. *All this time I thought I'd be killed for being a third child. Instead, I'm going to be killed for being in the Population Police. Isn't irony fun?*

"Reinforcements are coming!" Trey screamed. "They'll have more food! *Good* food! They won't give it to you if you hurt me!"

Nobody was fooled. Hands were still reaching for him. Fists, too. Trey squirmed away and dived through the crowd. It was just like playing Red Rover back at Hendricks School—everything hurt, but he broke through. He landed in a heap on the ground, and immediately scrambled up and took off running.

"Get him!" somebody yelled.

Trey ran faster than he'd ever run before. He could hear the crowd behind him, roaring. Once or twice a hand wrapped around his arm, but he always managed to shake it off.

"Help!" he called. "Help!"

And then he didn't have enough air to spare for yelling. He just kept running and running and running, blindly forcing his body on long after he felt like his lungs would explode and his legs would crumble and his heart would thump itself apart. He was too terrified to look back to see if the mob was gaining on him. He crashed into brush, and it felt enough like running into the woods back at Hendricks that he just kept going. Then he landed in water.

He couldn't swim.

"Uhb, hel—" he sputtered, too breathless even to call for help. He struggled back to the shoreline and clutched a rock for safety. He was too exhausted to pull himself out right away. He waited for someone to push him back in, to kill him by drowning rather than beating.

It took him a few minutes to realize the mob was far behind him. He could hear them calling in the distance, "Where is he? Where'd he go?"

I outran them, he thought, astonished. It was all because Lee had taught him how to run back at Hendricks.

Of course, how much of an accomplishment is it to out-run people who are starving to death? he reminded himself.

On shaking legs, he stood up. He was lost now. Except—this was the river, wasn't it? Could he just continue along the shore? In which direction?

He looked from side to side, up and down the river. In the distance, he could see a dimly lit bridge. Was that the bridge near where he and Mark had hidden the truck? Or had he already run past that bridge, past the truck? What if he took too long finding it?

He took off toward the bridge, rushing through the weeds and brush. A branch lashed across his face, and brambles tore at his uniform, but he kept going. It was much harder walking along the river without Mark ahead of him, clearing the way.

He was so intent on just moving forward and dodging branches that he practically ran into the concrete side of the bridge.

"Uff," he grunted.

He looked up. Two lanterns stood on posts on either side of the bridge, casting feeble light into the wisps of fog rising from the river. He heard footsteps, but it was only a sentry pacing from one side of the bridge to the other. Trey could see the Population Police insignia on the sentry's sleeve, and he relaxed.

How can I be relieved to see the Population Police? he wondered.

He just didn't want to face another mob.

Backing blindly away from the bridge, he felt around in all directions, desperately hoping that his hand would brush a hubcap or a fender. But there was no truck hidden here.

"No," Trey moaned. The muscles in his legs began to tremble, exhaustion and panic catching up with him. If he didn't find the truck soon, he had no hope of rescuing Mark. Why had he agreed to such an impossible plan? How could he possibly find the truck now?

He peered up and down the river once again, looking for another bridge. Why hadn't he paid closer attention when he and Mark were hiding the truck? Why hadn't he memorized every detail of their surroundings? Why wasn't it daylight so he could see better?

No, he didn't want it to be daylight. When it was daylight, Mark would die.

In desperation, Trey looked around yet again. This time, when he was swinging his head back and forth, he caught a glimpse of something shiny on the opposite shore—

metal, or maybe glass, catching the dim reflection of the lanterns on the bridge.

Trey locked his head in place and stared. Maybe, maybe . . .

What if this was the right bridge, but the truck was on the opposite side?

Trey squinted, trying to turn the small gleam into an entire truck, tucked away under leaves and branches.

Did I cross a bridge over the river? Could I have done that without noticing?

Of course he could have—when he was running away from the mob, or even before, when he was trying to stay in the shadows. He remembered the way Mark had taunted him, "I think if I'd never seen the outdoors, I'd keep my eyes open once I was in it." Trey's not paying attention had almost cost Mark his life.

And it still might turn out to.

Trey stepped tentatively back into the water, but it was cold and the current rushed at him. The riverbed sloped so severely that he could tell: Only a few more steps and the water would be over his head.

Why hadn't Lee included swimming in the roster of athletics he pushed at us back at Hendricks? Trey thought ruefully.

But he hadn't, and there was no time to waste regretting that now.

Trey was going to have to cross the bridge.

CHAPTER *TWENTY-FIVE*

alt! Who goes there?"

Trey had barely begun climbing up toward the bridge before the sentry began yelling at him. He had practically forgotten about the sentry. He'd been more worried about the lights.

"No one's allowed to cross this bridge!" the sentry screamed. "Turn back or be shot!"

"Relax," Trey said, remembering how well bluffing had worked before. "I'm a Population Police guard come to, uh, requisition a contraband vehicle parked over there." He pointed at the opposite shore and then, for good measure, lifted his arm to show the insignia on his sleeve. But now that he was in the light, he saw that the insignia was hanging by two threads from a ripped place in his sleeve. His pants were ripped too, he noticed, and mud stains covered the uniform from his waist down.

The sentry regarded him suspiciously.

"A mob attacked me," Trey said. "They thought I had food."

"No mob would dare lay a finger on a Population Police official," the sentry sniffed.

"This one did," Trey muttered.

"Where's your travel pass?" the sentry asked.

"Look, I've got authorizations," Trey said, reaching into his shirt pocket. But the authorizations only concerned transporting prisoners. The guard back at the Grants' house hadn't known that Trey would need authorization to cross this particular bridge.

The guard was reaching for Trey's papers. Any minute now he'd discover that Trey was a fraud.

"See? Now out of my way. I'm in a hurry," Trey said, shoving the papers back into his pocket.

"Wait! I couldn't—"

Trey took off in a dead run past the sentry.

"Stop! I have to sign the authorization!" the sentry was shouting behind him.

Trey reached the edge of the bridge and took a flying leap over the railing as soon as he saw firm ground on the other side. Except that it wasn't so firm—he began slipping and sliding down the mound of dirt, crashing through branches and leaves.

He stopped only when he slammed into the truck's tire.

Trey resisted the urge to hug the tire in relief and just lie there for a while. Instead, he scrambled up immediately, jerked open the door of the truck, and jumped inside, jamming the keys into the ignition. He'd planned to spend a few minutes studying all the dials on the dashboard, maybe reading the owner's manual from the glove compartment. But there wasn't time for that now. He turned the key.

Nothing happened.

Oops. What was that pedal I was supposed to push— the clutch?

He tried the key again, this time stabbing his feet at the pedals on the floor. The engine roared to life, but died while Trey was reaching for the gearshift.

Behind him, the sentry was leaning over the edge of the bridge, screaming at him.

"Sir! I insist—"

Trey ignored him, and concentrated on coordinating his feet and the gearshift. The truck lurched forward, toward the river.

No! No! Reverse! his mind screamed, and he shifted, grinding the gears horribly. The engine started to die again, and he panicked, hitting the gas pedal as hard as he could. The truck raced backward up the hill, toward the road. Branches scraped at the side of the truck and saplings broke off beneath the tires, but Trey didn't care as long as none of the obstacles stopped him.

The truck died again at the top of the hill, as Trey was trying to shift gears into forward.

"Sir! You are forcing me to conclude that you are not on a legitimate Population Police mission!" the sentry yelled at him. "Get out of that truck or—"

Trey started up the truck's engine yet again, and

zoomed past the sentry, going as fast as he could in first gear. The engine made a terrible noise, but Trey couldn't take the chance of trying to shift into second.

"I warned you!" the sentry screamed.

Trey heard gunfire, but nothing struck him, and nothing struck the truck as far as he could tell. He rounded a corner onto a new street, so that a row of buildings now stood between him and the sentry.

What if he radios for help? Trey wondered. *What if every Population Police official in the country starts looking for me?*

Trey pulled into a dark alleyway and shut off the engine. It was torture not to *know*. He silently crept back toward the bridge, staying hidden in the shadows the entire way.

The sentry was still standing on the bridge, but he wasn't screaming into a radio. For some strange reason, he was taking his shirt off. Puzzled, Trey watched as the sentry lay the shirt on the ground, walked a few paces away, and fired his gun at it. Then he put the gun away and held the shirt up in the air. Light shone through the gunshot holes in the front and back. Then, laughing, the sentry tossed the shirt over the edge of the bridge and waved at something or someone in the shadows on the other side. Several dark shapes emerged from the shadows—men in dark shirts and pants, all carrying huge bags on their shoulders. The bags appeared to be burlap, or some similar material meant for holding food.

Food? Were these smugglers?

The shirtless sentry tucked his gun into his waistband and grabbed a bag of his own. Then all of the men disappeared into the dark, walking in the opposite direction from Trey.

Did the sentry just desert from the Population Police? Trey wondered. *Or was he only pretending to begin with?*

Either way, he didn't seem worried about chasing down Trey, now that Trey was out of sight. Feeling vastly relieved, Trey crept back to the truck, started it, and began driving cautiously back to the Population Police headquarters.

After everything Trey had witnessed out in the streets, who could say what awaited him there?

etting back to the Grants' old house took only a frac-
tion of the time it'd taken to get to the truck. But the
whole time, Trey worried about the noise of the engine; he
worried about another mob swamping him. He worried
every time he accidentally killed the engine trying to shift
gears and had to struggle to restart it. Every time that
happened, he knew he was a sitting duck, a perfect target
for anyone who might happen along. But nobody
appeared.

Maybe the truck noise scares them off, Trey tried to tell
himself. *Maybe it's good I'm making so much racket.*

Between the mob, the smugglers, and the easily fooled
Population Police patrol, nothing seemed to fit with the
strictly regimented world his parents had always
described.

Has everything changed? Trey wondered. *Is everything
still changing?*

He peered into the area illuminated by his headlights as

if the air itself might suddenly become different.

Hey, Dad? he thought. *There's no way you could have prepared me for all of this. I know you did the best you could.*

The sky was still blessedly dark when Trey pulled up to the gates of the Population Police headquarters. The sentry guarding the gates yawned over Trey's authorization forms, and barely glanced at Trey.

"Permission granted to proceed," he mumbled.

Trey drove around to the back, hoping that he could manage not to kill the engine yet again right in front of headquarters. The truck did die a few feet away from the servants' door, but Trey decided to pretend that he'd parked there on purpose. The guard Mark and Trey had bargained with came rushing over immediately.

"Great!" he said. "Help me get the cage."

Trey followed him through the door and down a dark hallway toward the basement stairs.

"Why don't you just unlock the cage and let Mark walk?" Trey asked.

The guard shook his head.

"Can't," he said. "Bring me back my friend, and then I'll give you the key to your friend's cage."

"That's mighty manipulative of you, isn't it?" Trey joked, though he'd already agreed to that part of the deal.

The guard gave Trey a warning look as they came up to another guard sitting at a desk.

"Hey, Stan," the first guard said to the second one. "This

guy just showed up with authorization to transfer our prisoner out to Nezeree."

"Huh?" the other guard—Stan?—said. "I thought he was going to be executed at dawn." He didn't sound like he cared. He sounded like Mark's life didn't matter any more than a gnat's or a flea's.

"Maybe they're doing the execution out there," the first guard said with a shrug, as if it didn't matter to him either.

Stan peered carefully at the authorization papers.

"'Should we call Commander Bresin and double-check?" he asked.

The first guard shrugged.

"You can if you want. I don't feel like getting in trouble for waking him up."

Stan seemed to be deliberating. He looked at the papers again. Trey sincerely hoped that every forged signature looked authentic. Then Stan looked at Trey.

"They let guards dress that sloppy out at Nezeree?" he asked.

Trey was suddenly conscious of the rips in his uniform, the dirt caked on his shoes, the mud streaked across his pants. And when had he lost his cap?

"Aw, Stan, they've got a rough crowd out there in Nezeree. He was trying to subdue one of their prisoners and . . ." The first guard shrugged, as if the rest of the explanation should be obvious.

"Remind me not to get transferred out there," Stan said. He handed two of the papers back to Trey and laid the others down on his desk. "If the documents say our prisoner's going to be transferred instead of executed, I guess he's got to go. Need help loading?"

"Thanks, but the two of us can handle it," the first guard said smoothly.

Trey followed him down the stairs. This time the guard hit the light switch. Mark gasped at first, then grinned when he saw Trey.

"Act like you still think you're about to die," the guard whispered.

Mark nodded, then began to flail about in his cage.

"No, no," he screamed.

"Quietly," the guard commanded.

Mark switched to making a horrified expression and tugging uselessly on his bars.

"That's better," the guard said. He picked up one end of the cage, and Trey took the other. It was a strain, but together they managed to carry the cage up the stairs. The other guard, Stan, stood aside and let them pass.

"You're signing off on the paperwork on this," he told the first guard. "I don't want nobody blaming me for nothing."

"No problem," the first guard said. "Why would anybody blame anybody for anything? All the documents are right there."

He and Trey continued carrying Mark on out to the truck. With great effort, they managed to hoist the cage into the truck bed. Too late, Trey thought that he should have faked weakness, forced the guard to let Mark out. But the guard probably wouldn't have. He probably would have just gotten Stan to help.

The guard handed Trey even more papers.

"These'll let you pick up my friend. Once the warden at Nezeree signs them, you'll be authorized to pick up your other friends, too. They're at the holding camp in Slahood. But I arranged these documents so you can't get your friends without picking up my friend first. If—if you try to double-cross me, in any way, I'll find out. You'll both be on the most-wanted list. You'll be shot on sight by any Population Police officer in the country."

"I understand," Trey said, trying not to think about it.

The guard looked at his watch.

"It's five thirty-three. The transfer order for picking up your friends expires at ten. Just like we agreed."

Trey wanted to bargain for another hour or two. What if the officials at Nezeree were slow delivering their prisoner? What if he couldn't drive fast enough?

"One more thing," the guard said. "Just to make it look legitimate, I wrote on these documents that all the prisoners you're transporting are being sent to Churko—the worst prison of all. So . . . don't let anyone else take over your delivery job." He laughed, but without any humor.

"Okay," Trey said. He slid back into the driver's seat. His knees were shaking, but he somehow managed to start the truck and shift it into reverse.

"Good luck," the guard said. He tilted his head to look

up at the truck, and his cap slid back on his head. For the first time, Trey got a good look at the guard's face in the glow from a security light overhead. The guard had kindly eyes that somehow looked familiar. And he was older than Trey had thought. Short gray hair spiked out from under his cap.

"*Liber,*" Trey whispered.

He thought he'd spoken too softly to be heard over the engine noise. But the guard answered him.

"Free," he whispered back. "God free us all."

CHAPTER *TWENTY-SEVEN*

T rey had barely driven out the gates of Population Police headquarters when Mark began tapping on the window behind him. Trey turned around to look, practically driving off the road in the process. He slammed on the brake just in time to avoid ending up in the ditch. Of course, that killed the engine instantly.

With shaking hands, Trey opened the window behind him so he could talk to Mark.

"Good grief! Who taught you how to drive?" Mark asked jokingly.

"You," Trey said.

"I think I was safer facing execution," Mark moaned.

"I'm doing the best I can," Trey muttered through gritted teeth. His heart was still pounding hard, though. What if they had landed in the ditch, gotten stuck, and missed their deadline for rescuing Lee and the others?

"Okay, here's what we do," Mark said. "There's a tool chest under the seat. Find the wire cutter in there, set me free, and then let's go straight to picking up Luke."

Trey glanced around quickly, as if he was afraid someone would hear. They were in a deserted stretch, but he'd already learned that deserted-looking areas might hold the most danger.

"You've got to be kidding," he whispered back to Mark. "Didn't you hear the guard? If we double-cross him—if we don't pick up his friend first—we can't get our friends, and we'll be shot on sight by any Population Police officer."

"What if he was just bluffing? What if this is all just a trap that's going to get us both killed—and Lee and the others, too?" Mark asked.

Trey hadn't considered that possibility. He'd been too focused on the challenges of getting to the right place at the right time.

"What if the guard's friend is dangerous?" Mark continued.

"I don't know," Trey wailed. The dashboard lights flickered. "Does that mean something bad?" he asked Mark.

"Yeah, you're starting to drain the battery. Look, just hand me the toolbox, and start the engine again and keep driving. Once I get out of here, I'll take over the wheel. Then you can look through the documents and see if you spot a trick."

In the dark, Trey searched around under the seat until he found a large metal box. He stepped out of the cab only long enough to put the toolbox in the truck bed beside the cage, well within Mark's reach. Mark handed him something round in exchange. Trey stared at it, puzzled.

"It's an apple," Mark said. "Remember? Food? The guard gave me my knapsack back. You've got to be at least as hungry as I am."

"Thanks," Trey said.

He slid back into the front seat, and took a bite. The apple seemed to be the most delicious food he'd ever tasted in his life.

Good thing that mob's not chasing me now, he thought, as he started the engine again and drove cautiously back onto the road.

He didn't understand how the Population Police could promise people food, and then not give it to them. Or just give them ruined food.

Aldous Krakenaur isn't running the Government very well, Trey thought, then almost giggled at the absurdity of it all. Of course Aldous Krakenaur wasn't running the government well. He was most concerned with killing people.

What if that was the guard's goal too?

Just drive, Trey told himself. *Don't think.*

The road that led toward both the Nezeree prison and the Slahood detention camp carried them away from the city after just a few miles, and Trey was heartily relieved. The countryside seemed much less threatening.

Trey left the back window of the truck open, and he could hear Mark muttering behind him.

". . . wire cutter's not strong enough, but maybe with the pliers—"

"Can't you hurry?" Trey shouted back at him.

"I'm doing the best I can," Mark yelled. "Just like you. But it'd help if you stopped weaving so much!"

Trey concentrated on driving in as straight a line as possible. But then the road swerved to the left, and he barely managed to turn in time.

"Hey!" Mark yelled. "Watch it!"

"Sorry," Trey said.

He slowed down for all the curves after that, which was frustrating. He didn't have a watch on, but he could feel each minute ticking by. The sky was starting to brighten a little directly ahead of him—to the east, he guessed.

It was five thirty-three when we left. Is it six o'clock now? Six thirty? And Mark's still in his cage and I'm scared to drive very fast . . . What if we don't get there in time?

The road got curvier. Mark seemed to have given up on trying to escape, and just focused on coaching Trey around each turn.

"Ease the clutch out gradually," he was saying as Trey maneuvered around a particularly narrow hairpin twist.

Trey was concentrating so completely on his shaking leg muscles that he didn't see what hit the opposite side of the truck. But he heard shrieking, and then Mark screamed behind him, "Speed up! We're under attack!"

In his panic, Trey let his foot slip off the clutch pedal

entirely. The truck died. Trey glanced quickly off to the right as he reached for the key to restart the engine. Dark shapes were swarming all over the truck. They began to rock it.

"Food! Food! We want food!" the crowd chanted, bouncing the truck up and down.

"Leave us alone!" Mark yelled.

The next thing Trey knew, the truck was turning over.

CHAPTER *TWENTY-EIGHT*

The truck landed on its side with enough force that the windshield shattered. Trey sat still, absolutely stunned, for several seconds, then unfastened his seat belt and shimmied out through the gaping hole in front of him.

Mark hadn't had a seat belt. His cage hadn't even been anchored down.

The mob had flowed around to the front of the truck, but nobody seemed to notice Trey escaping.

"An apple core!" somebody screamed. Trey's must have fallen out onto the dirt by the side of the road. The whole crowd gathered around and seemed to be fighting over what little flesh still remained around the seeds.

Trey slipped around toward the back, and, in the dark-ness, practically tripped over Mark's overturned cage. He felt around inside the bars, even though he was terrified that he might find only a dead body.

"Mark?" he called. "Mark?"

"Over here," a voice called behind him.

Trey rushed over to a huge rock beside the road. Mark was crouched there.

"How—?" Trey couldn't make himself understand. "What happened? Why aren't you in the cage?"

"Cage busted open when it hit the ground," Mark whispered.

"Really? That's great!" Trey said, not even fazed by the wacky grammar of "busted open." It seemed downright miraculous that the mob had actually helped them.

"Yeah," Mark said. "But my leg busted open too."

Trey reached down, his fingers brushing sticky blood.

"Don't," Mark said. "I think the bone's poking out a little. You probably shouldn't touch it."

"People with open fractures aren't supposed to be moved," Trey remembered from a phase when his dad had had him memorize all sorts of first aid information.

"What was I supposed to do—lie there and let those people trample me?" Mark hissed. He winced, and for the first time Trey realized that Mark was in intense pain.

"We should wrap it until we can get you to a doctor," Trey said.

"Uh-huh," Mark said, grimacing. Trey eased Mark's arms out of his flannel shirt, and wrapped the shirt around Mark's leg. But this was crazy—how would they ever get him to a doctor?

"You go on," Mark said through gritted teeth. "Go get Luke before it's too late."

"But—," Trey started to argue.

"You'll have to walk from here," Mark said. "I don't think it's much farther."

Trey stared out at the mob, still swarming around the truck. They'd discovered the knapsack now, and were fighting over it like a bunch of wild animals. How long before they decided to come looking for Mark and Trey?

Trey looked down again at his injured friend. The choice before him now was not between cowardice and bravery. Whether he stayed to take care of Mark or left to rescue Lee and his other friends—as well as the guard's mysterious prisoner—Trey would need immense courage. How was he supposed to choose?

"Go," Mark moaned.

"No," Trey said. He looked back and forth between Mark and the mob again. "Just a minute."

He took his Population Police shirt off and dropped it beside Mark. Then he stepped out from behind the rock and joined the mob.

"Gimme some! Gimme some!" he snarled, just like the others were doing. He pushed and shoved, reaching toward the backpack.

A boy beside him—also shirtless—glanced toward Trey but said nothing, only elbowed him out of the way.

"Wait! Wait! It rolled under the truck!" Trey screamed.

He rushed over to the truck and began pushing uselessly against the cab top.

"*Lots* of food rolled under the truck!" he screamed again.

A few members of the crowd joined him, shoving against the truck as well, trying to set it back up on its tires.

"Oranges! Bananas! All under the truck!" Trey yelled. Then he worried that someone might ask him how a banana might roll—or how anything could roll under a truck lying flat on its side. But nobody said anything, except to grunt in exertion. The mob was too hungry for logic. Even more people joined him, pushing and pushing on the truck. With one great shove, they had it upright again.

A cheer burst forth, and everyone instantly fell to the ground, feeling around for the promised oranges and bananas. Everyone, that is, except Trey. He backed away, then took off running down the road, toward one of the curves he'd navigated right before being attacked by the mob.

"Truck alert!" he yelled once he was sure he was out of sight. "It's—ooh, it looks like a whole truckful of bread. It's loaded! Come and help stop it! Come and eat!"

For a second, Trey was afraid his trick wouldn't work. Even though the sun was beginning to rise, it was still too dark to see what a truck down the road might be loaded with. But then he heard the trample of feet behind him. He circled around, hiding behind rocks and trees as the mob passed him. Then he took off sprinting toward Mark.

"What?" Mark murmured. "What are you doing?"

Trey grabbed his Population Police shirt back and stuffed his arms into the sleeves, then grabbed Mark under the armpits and dragged him toward the now-upright truck.

"Ooooh," Mark moaned, the most agonizing sound Trey had ever heard. Then Mark's body went limp. Had he passed out from the pain? Trey didn't take the time to check. He jerked open the truck door and hoisted Mark into the cab, then slid in beside him.

The keys were still in the ignition. Trey reached for them.

"It may not start," Mark moaned beside him. So he was conscious, after all. "After being flipped like that, some of the wires might have been scrambled, the engine case cracked or something. . . ."

Trey turned the key, and the engine sputtered to life.

"Good old Bessie," Mark muttered. "I'll never talk bad about this truck again."

Trey eased off the clutch as gently as possible. He shifted through the gears like a pro.

When he got to fourth gear, he floored the gas pedal, and the truck zoomed toward the dawn, air streaming into the cab from every direction.

CHAPTER *TWENTY-NINE*

They arrived at the Nezeree prison fifteen minutes later. Trey slowed down approaching the gates.

"We'll pick up the guard's friend first," he told Mark. "I think we have to play by his rules even if . . . even if it might be a trick."

Trey was kind of hoping that Mark would challenge him, offer some other brilliant plan. But Mark just moaned in response. It was light enough now that Trey could see the pallor of Mark's face, the bloodstains on the shirt wrapped around his leg.

"Maybe the guard's friend will be a doctor who can set your leg for you," Trey joked halfheartedly.

"Chains," Mark muttered.

"Huh?"

"Chains . . . under the seat," Mark said. "Put them around my wrists to make it look like . . ."

"Oh. So you'll look like a prisoner," Trey finished, to spare Mark the effort of talking. After an anxious glance in

MARGARET PETERSON HADDIX

his rearview mirror to make sure there was no mob ready to pounce again, he pulled over to the side of the road, dug around under the seat, and pulled out a length of chain, which he draped across Mark's body. Mark held his right hand off to the side.

"What's this?" Trey said, staring at a painful-looking wound on the palm of Mark's hand.

"Burns," Mark said through gritted teeth. "From the electric fence. Got some on my back, too."

"Why didn't you tell me?"

"No time," Mark groaned. "Hurry up."

Trey was careful not to place any of the links directly on Mark's leg or burns, but Mark still groaned in pain.

"Heavy," Mark muttered. Beads of sweat glistened along his hairline, but he was shivering. Trey struggled to remember: Could somebody die from a broken leg? And was Mark still in danger from touching the electric fence the day before?

He pushed those worries to the back of his mind and drove on up to the gates of the prison. They stood between tall walls of chain-link fence topped with loops of razor wire.

"Not another prisoner coming in," the guard on duty griped when he glanced into the truck.

"No, no," Trey said soothingly. "I'm picking up one of your prisoners. Then I'm taking both of them to Churko."

He was relieved that the guard seemed to accept him as a Population Police officer and Mark as a prisoner—in spite of their ragged appearance, in spite of the smashed-up truck. Trey held the authorization papers out the window. The guard looked through them and handed them right back.

"Warden's office is straight ahead on the right," he said.

"Thanks," Trey said.

"Warden's a stickler for appearances, if you know what I mean," the guard said.

"Oh," Trey said.

"I'm just warning you, that's all," the guard said. "He likes spit-polished shoes."

Trey glanced down at the mud flaking off his shoes, the stains and rips arcing across his pant legs.

"Got an extra uniform I can borrow, then?" Trey asked.

The guard shook his head, grinning.

"Good luck," he said, like it was all a joke.

Great, Trey thought. *Mark's almost passing out from pain, I may be walking into a trap, I still don't know if I can save Lee and Nina and the others in time—and this guy thinks it's funny that I'm going to get yelled at for not spit-polishing my shoes.*

Or maybe I won't be able to save Lee and Nina and the others—or Mark—just because my shoes aren't spit-polished. . . .

Thinking hard, Trey drove on to the warden's office. It was a small, tidy building, with flowers planted along the walkway. A boy about Trey's age—but wearing a much neater uniform—was scrubbing the windows. Behind the office, dozens of official-looking Population Police cars and trucks and buses gleamed in the early-morning sunlight. They looked like they'd each been polished with a toothbrush; they looked like someone had used a ruler to make sure all the vehicles were parked at exactly the same intervals.

Trey let the engine of his truck die several feet back from a concrete divider in front of the warden's office. It was his best parking attempt yet, but his tires still overlapped the white lines marking his space.

That was the least of his worries.

"I'll be back as soon as I can," Trey told Mark.

Mark nodded, and seemed to turn a few shades paler.

Trey got out of the truck and walked to the front door of the warden's office. He rapped his knuckles against the wood frame, trying to make his knock sound precise and official.

"Enter," a voice called.

Trey took a deep breath, then opened the door and stepped in onto luxurious-looking carpet. A man in a heavily decorated uniform sat behind a huge mahogany desk. Trey reminded himself he didn't have time to stare at all the man's ribbons and medals.

"Sir!" Trey barked, snapping his arm into a salute against his capless forehead. "Officer Jackson reporting. Request permission to present papers."

The man looked bemused.

"At ease," he said. "Proceed."

"I must first offer apologies for my appearance, sir!" Trey said.

The man looked him up and down, a slight frown playing across his heavyset face.

"Apologize, then," he said.

"Sir!" Trey repeated yet again. "I am a disgrace to the honor of this uniform." He remembered the excuse the guard had given back at the Grants' house. "I was subduing a prisoner who had no proper respect for Population Police authority. I know it is no excuse, but that is why my uniform is ripped and I am covered in mud. And I lost my cap. I am deeply ashamed to appear before you like this."

"Indeed," the man said. But he was smiling now. "I wish the guards in my unit shared your concerns. You did succeed in subduing the prisoner, though?"

"Yes, sir," Trey said. On the theory that a smidgen of truth strengthened any lie, he added, "I broke his leg, sir. I believe he may be on the verge of death."

"Well done," the man said.

Trey barely managed not to gag with revulsion at that. How could this man care so much about spit-polished shoes and so little about a human life?

The man glanced out the window, to where Mark sat in chains.

"This prisoner is being transferred into my jurisdiction?" he asked.

"No, sir," Trey said. His arm was beginning to ache from saluting for so long, but he kept it in position. "I am picking up one of your prisoners and taking both of them on to Churko."

The warden motioned for Trey to give him the paper-work. He looked through the papers, seeming to read each one carefully.

"You're taking prisoners from Slahood as well? That's odd . . . ," he murmured.

"I'm only following orders, sir!" Trey said, hoping to distract him.

The warden narrowed his eyes, looking straight at Trey. Trey worried that he had carried his act too far. He'd been trying to behave like a groveling flunky had in a military book he'd once read. How did he know how Population Police officials talked in real life?

Then the warden said, "I like your attitude, young man. Are you a new recruit?"

Just in case the warden had some way of checking, Trey told the truth.

"Yes, sir! I joined up yesterday, sir!" Had it only been yesterday that he'd stood in that long line at the Grant house? It seemed many, many lifetimes ago.

"The new recruits I've been sent lack your enthusiasm for our cause. They seem most concerned about eating," the warden sneered. It seemed like an unfair gibe, consid-ering that the warden must have weighed more than two hundred and fifty pounds—he'd obviously spent a lot of time himself being concerned about eating. "Any chance I could have you transferred to my unit?"

Oh, great, Trey thought. *I've played my part too well.*

"Sir?" Trey said cautiously. "I would not want to be dis-loyal to my current commander. I must finish my assignment before I could think of being transferred."

"Of course," the warden said. "I should have known you'd have that response." He tidied Trey's papers into a single stack. "Here's what I'll do. I'll have one of my guards go pick up the prisoners from Slahood right now. That will save you quite a bit of time. I'll have another guard retrieve prisoner"—he glanced down at Trey's forms—"prisoner 908653 from cell block three here at Nezeree. And I'll have a fresh uniform sent up for you to change into while you're waiting." The warden barked a few short commands into an intercom on his desk, and it was all set in motion.

"Thank you, sir," Trey said, unable to believe his good luck.

"And the prisoner in the truck," the warden said. "I'll write up an order to have him shot right now."

"What?" The luxurious room seemed to be spinning slightly. Surely Trey hadn't heard the warden properly. Surely his brilliant lies hadn't led to this.

"For attacking a Population Police officer," the warden said casually. "It's a capital offense, you know."

And he reached for a pen.

CHAPTER *THIRTY*

The room was truly spinning now. Mark was the one being sentenced to death, but it was Trey whose life flashed before his eyes. How could he have done this? How could he have rescued Mark—twice—only to see him killed here, now, just as he was about to be reunited with his brother?

"No!" Trey exploded.

"What did you just say to me?" the warden asked, his pen hesitating over the paper.

"I mean, 'No, *sir*'. I mean—" Trey scrambled to think. "The prisoner certainly deserves to die. Not because he attacked me, but because he showed no respect for me, as an officer of the Population Police. Still . . . the warden at Churko has personal reasons for wanting to . . . to torture this particular prisoner. And for wanting to oversee his death himself."

"Ah," the warden said. He seemed to be considering. "I see." He reached for a different paper from one of the stacks on his desk. "Then I'll order that our infirmary sets his leg and gives him medicine. So that he lives long enough for my colleague at Churko to see him tortured."

Trey watched in awe as the warden scribbled out an order and summoned an underling over the intercom on his desk.

What kind of person is willing to kill or save a boy's life on a whim, just like that? Trey wondered. *What kind of government allows someone to have that kind of power, all by himself?*

A uniformed guard showed up at the door and entered without speaking. The warden looked at him disapprovingly.

"Nedley, drive this man's vehicle over to the infirmary and have his prisoner treated there," the warden said. "Officer Jackson, you can give him your keys."

"I—I feel responsible for the prisoner, sir," Trey said. "I'll drive him there myself, if you just tell me where to go."

"Oh, no," the warden said. "Son, you need to learn about chain of command. Mark my words, you're going to advance high up in the Population Police, and you need to learn to delegate. Nedley—do as I say!"

Trey saw no choice but to hold the keys out to the silent Nedley.

What's going to happen when they discover that Mark isn't really chained up? Trey wondered. *What if this is all a trick? What's Mark going to do when this strange offi-cer climbs into the truck?*

But that last worry, at least, proved unnecessary. Trey

glanced out the window and could see: Mark appeared to have passed out from the pain once again.

"Oh, and Nedley?" the warden was continuing. "Gas up his vehicle before you bring it back."

"Yes, sir," Nedley said in a dispirited voice.

Trey watched anxiously as Nedley climbed into the truck, started it, and pulled away. The warden misread Trey's concern.

"So good to see a young recruit taking his responsibilities seriously," the warden mumbled. "I *will* request that you be transferred here after you deliver your prisoners to Churko. This is a much more prestigious posting. See this phone here?" He pointed to a dark, heavy phone that seemed to occupy a place of honor in the center of his spotless desk. "I've got a direct, secure line that goes straight to Population Police headquarters. I'm talking to the highest-level officials constantly. Out at Churko—bah! I bet half the time headquarters forgets they're there."

"Your status is impressive, sir," Trey said politely, though he was distracted worrying about Mark, worrying about Lee and the others, worrying about the mysterious prisoner he was supposed to take back to the guard at Population Police headquarters.

We don't need that prisoner to trade for the key to Mark's cage anymore, Trey realized with a jolt. *If I can get all of us out of here safely, what should we do with the extra prisoner? Leave him by the side of the road for the mobs to attack?*

And then Trey felt a wave of shame. He was thinking like a true Population Police officer, seeing human life as disposable. He swayed slightly, suddenly feeling faint.

The warden was still talking about the glories of the Nezeree prison.

"We're a model for the entire system, I tell you—oh, just put it over there. Dismissed."

An aide had come in with a new uniform for Trey. The warden glanced at his watch as the aide put the uniform down on a chair and silently departed.

"It's time for my morning inspection of the barracks," the warden said. "I am never late. Tell you what. You go back into my personal quarters and take a shower and change. Have some breakfast, too, if you like. I'll be back momentarily. And we'll have those prisoners ready for you in a flash."

"Yes, sir," Trey said. He picked up the clean clothes and went through the door the warden indicated. But his legs were rubbery, and his mind felt equally numb.

What are they doing to Mark right now, while I'm getting a nice, hot shower? How long until Lee gets here? What if we can't pull this off?

A tiny, tiny part of his brain suggested slipping out the nearest window and finding a place to hide, but he ignored that impulse. He undressed and stepped into the shower instead, turning the water on full blast.

If they see through my bluff, at least I'll die clean, Trey thought bitterly. *The warden would like that.*

The hot water did seem to clear his brain. For the first time he noticed that the water faucet handles were pure crystal, the showerhead was shiny brass. After he'd toweled off and gotten dressed again, he used the towel to wipe out the expensive-looking tiles of the shower floor and walls. He soaked up every last drop of water so it looked as though the shower had never been used. The last thing he needed was to upset the warden over something stupid like a messy shower. He deliberated about what to do with his old, filthy uniform, and finally tucked it into a waste can hidden under the sink.

He was halfway out the bathroom door when he remembered the Grants' and the Talbots' papers, still tucked in the old uniform's pockets.

Surely they don't matter now, he thought. He was dangerously close to thinking that nothing else mattered either, that he and his friends were doomed, regardless. But he forced himself to turn around anyway and rescue the papers yet again. He stuffed them into a hidden pocket in his new uniform.

If I can save the papers, maybe I can save my friends, too, he told himself superstitiously.

And then he was antsy, wandering from room to room, fretting about when the warden would come back, when Mark would reappear, when the prisoners would arrive.

How bizarre, Trey thought. *I don't know how to sit still anymore.*

He forced himself to choke down two English muffins and a bowl of cereal in the small but well-stocked kitchenette, but it was more out of necessity than desire. Though he knew he needed the energy, he couldn't force himself to concentrate even on food.

When he was up and wandering again, he noticed voices coming from behind a closed door just down the hallway from the warden's office. Thinking the warden had returned—or that maybe his friends had finally arrived—he leaned toward the door to listen.

". . . at the top of our news . . . ," a voice was saying.

Television? Trey thought.

He knocked lightly. When no one answered, he turned the knob and opened the door a crack. The television was speaking to an empty roomful of chairs. Trey eased into one of them.

The warden wouldn't get upset about me watching TV, would he? Trey wondered.

The last time Trey had seen a television, he'd learned about the Population Police overthrowing the government. So he regarded this one uneasily.

"Our glorious leader gave an enormously well-received speech to the populace last evening," a man was saying, over footage of Aldous Krakenaur standing with raised fists before a huge cheering crowd.

Where are the starving people begging for food? Trey wondered.

Feeling antsy again, he got up and began flipping

through channels. The same footage was on the first four stations. The fifth channel was Krakenaur again, but alone at a desk in a room Trey recognized as Krakenaur's office at Population Police headquarters. A tag line at the bottom of the screen read, "Population Police Official Network."

It made sense: If the Barons had their own stations, why shouldn't the Population Police?

Krakenaur was staring into the camera—and, it seemed, out at Trey—with frightening intensity.

"These five men were caught smuggling last night," Krakenaur was saying. He held up a handful of pictures. The camera zoomed in to focus on each face individually.

Peering into the TV screen, Trey gasped. The first picture was the sentry from the bridge the night before. He guessed that the others were the men he'd seen carrying bags across the bridge the night before. Except, in the pictures, they were all dead.

"They were stealing food from our citizens," Krakenaur was saying, icily. The camera focused on him again. "Death is too good for traitors like these. From now on, smugglers will be executed on sight. In my eyes, they are as vile and offensive as third children."

Someone off-camera handed Krakenaur a sheet of paper. He glanced down to read it. Just from the small bits of televised news he'd seen before, Trey suspected that in a regular newscast the camera would have switched to someone else or some other footage. Watching a man read a note would have been considered dead airtime. But the camera stayed trained on Krakenaur, as if it might be treason to focus elsewhere without his permission.

When Krakenaur finally looked up, his eyes seemed even colder and harder, and his voice was filled with even icier fury.

"I have just been informed of other traitors," he said. "A father and son, working in our midst. Population Police officers—trusted, respected, given great responsibility. And they have betrayed us! They have betrayed us all!" He pounded his fist on his desk. Trey flinched as if he were right there in the same room with Krakenaur's rising wrath. As if Krakenaur's fist were hitting *him*.

"Jonas Sabine and his son Jonathan will be executed as soon as we finish interrogating them," Krakenaur said. "I am hereby instructing all Population Police officials to disregard all orders from Jonas or Jonathan Sabine. Hold all documents they have signed, and detain anyone carrying documents with their signatures. We are tracing the extent of their treachery, even as I speak. We'll be notifying everyone involved as soon as possible." Then he addressed someone off-camera. "Do we have pictures?"

Trey heard a muffed "Yes, sir" and "Right away, sir," and a crashing sound, as if someone had knocked over a chair scrambling to obey Krakenaur. A hand slipped pictures onto his desk, and he held them up in front of the camera.

"All Population Police officers must report all conversations and encounters they've had with these two men,"

Krakenaur was saying as the camera zoomed in. "Or else you will be considered traitors too."

The pictures came slowly into focus. The son's photo was first: a freckle-faced boy with a jaunty smile and features that Trey recognized instantly.

"Liber," Trey whispered.

It was the boy who had found Trey on the Talbots' porch, the boy who had saved Trey's life by telling him to hide instead of reporting him. One of only two Population Police officials that Trey had ever heard speak of freedom.

Trey felt a horrible sense of dread rising in his gut.

When the father's picture appeared, he was not surprised. It was a man with gray hair and eyes that looked familiar—familiar because they matched his son's. Trey had noticed the resemblance only the night before, but not quite made the connection.

It was the Population Police guard from the Grants' house. The one who had arranged all the documents Trey had brought to Nezeree.

"Disregard all orders from Jonas or Jonathan Sabine," Krakenaur had said. "Hold all documents they have signed, and detain anyone carrying documents with their signatures. We are tracing the extent of their treachery, even as I speak. We'll be notifying everyone involved as soon as possible."

Could Trey and his friends escape Nezeree before the warden found out?

Distantly, Trey heard a phone ringing in another room. As if in a trance, he stumbled out of the TV room toward the ominous sound. He tripped into the warden's office, and it was exactly as Trey feared: The phone on the warden's desk was ringing. The one that was a direct line to Population Police headquarters.

MARGARET PETERSON HADDIX

CHAPTER *THIRTY-ONE*

T rey dived under the warden's desk and yanked the phone cord out of the wall. He wished he had a knife. But he didn't, so he put the plastic tip of the cord in his mouth and sawed it against his teeth. Finally, finally, he managed to bite off the end, leaving the wires frayed.

"What is the meaning of this?" a voice exploded behind him.

Trey spit out the plastic connector and hid the phone cord deep in the carpet. He backed out and slowly straightened up. The warden was just coming in the door. What had he seen? What had he heard?

"C-c-cockroach, sir," Trey stammered. "I'm so sorry. I saw this bug running behind your desk, and I know how those things multiply, and I thought if I caught it—"

"Did you?" the warden asked.

"No, sir. I wasn't fast enough. I'm sorry, sir."

The warden regarded Trey doubtfully. What if he decided to get down on his hands and knees to look for himself?

He won't, Trey tried to assure himself. *He's too fat to fit.*

The warden glanced down at his desk. Was Trey being paranoid, or was the warden looking straight at his phone? *Had* he heard it ringing?

A printerlike machine behind Trey began churning out paper.

"Looks like I'm getting a fax," the warden said. "Step aside, Officer Jackson. It's undoubtedly classified, and you wouldn't have clearance yet to see that."

There was a challenging note to his voice, but Trey took hope from the word "yet."

He still thinks I'm a gung-ho Population Police recruit, Trey thought. *He still thinks I'll have classified clearance someday.*

"Here, sir, I'll get the fax for you," Trey said. "I won't look at it. I promise."

He did his best to sound earnest and overeager, not like a boy who was terrified of what that fax might say. But he didn't have to look to know. "We'll be notifying everyone involved as soon as possible," Krakenaur had said. The phone call had failed, so of course the Population Police were using other methods.

"All right," the warden said in an even tone. But he was watching Trey carefully.

The fax machine kept spitting out paper. Trey stood waiting, his hands over the machine, the dread growing inside him. Should he rip the papers in half when he picked them up? Should he run away with them? How could he do anything about the fax without giving himself away—and destroying any chance that Mark, Lee, and the others had for escape?

But what chance do any of us have anymore anyway? Trey wondered in despair.

The last sheet of paper churned out, and the machine lapsed into silence. Trey reached down and scooped up the papers. Without looking, he thumped them against the counter, straightening out the edges.

Do I dare to drop them? Buy myself a little time?

But he was too nervous to try that, and too scared of infuriating the warden.

The noise of a truck outside distracted him temporarily.

"Your prisoners from Slahood have arrived," the warden said, glancing out the window.

Trey let the hand holding the papers fall to his side. He rushed over to the window as if his eagerness to see his prisoners had made him forget about the fax.

"We were giving our prisoner one last beating before he leaves," the warden said. He leaned over and spoke into the intercom, "Snyder, you may send him up now."

Trey peered out the window as a truck pulled up in front of the warden's office. Lee, Nina, Joel, and John were chained together in the back. So was a fifth person, a man.

The chauffeur? Trey suddenly thought. He hadn't recognized him at first, because the chauffeur looked twenty years older than he had the last time Trey had seen him, back at the Talbots' house only a week or so earlier. *Mark and I didn't ask to have the chauffeur released,* Trey thought. *We didn't even mention his name. We don't even know his name.*

The chauffeur's appearance only intensified Trey's fears. Everything was spinning out of control, even without the danger presented by the fax papers burning in his hand.

"I'll go help unload the prisoners," Trey said.

"But my fax—young man! You haven't been dismissed!" the warden yelled from behind him.

Trey pretended not to hear, though it was a shaky pretense. He would have had to be deaf to miss those shouts. He rushed out the door anyway. How long would it take the warden to catch up to him? A minute? Two? Would the warden pause to summon other guards over the intercom—guards who would come to beat him up?

Trey tried not to think about it.

Outside, the driver from Slahood was already jerking Trey's friends and the chauffeur out of the truck bed. They stumbled and fell, knocking against one another. But the guard gave them no time to right themselves, just kept pulling on their chains until they were all in a heap on the ground.

None of them so much as cried out in pain.

"Who's signing for this riffraff?" the guard asked.

"Me," Trey said, blindly grabbing for the clipboard and pen the guard held out. He scrawled his most illegible signature at the bottom of the forms.

"Okay, then," the guard said, and climbed back into his truck and drove away.

Trey knew he should be running, putting as much distance as he could between himself and the warden. Using every last second to save himself. But time seemed to stop as he stood there regarding his friends. They lay like corpses at his feet, not making the least attempt to untangle themselves. He wasn't sure if they recognized him or not.

"Everything's okay now," he wanted to tell them. "I'm rescuing you." But he knew that would be a lie—he had no hope of carrying off a rescue now. Failing that, Trey at least wanted to ask some questions: "Why did you leave me? Why did you go back to the Grants' house? Why didn't you come back for me?"

But it was too late for questions. The warden came storming out of his office, screaming, "Give me that fax this instant!"

At the same time, the guard who had taken Mark away, Nedley, was pulling up in Mark's battered truck. Mark sat in the passenger's seat, looking groggy but blessedly alive—for now, anyway. A body also lay in the back, but Trey couldn't tell if he was looking at a corpse or at a living, breathing human.

That must be the prisoner that Jonas Sabine risked his life for. Wonder why Sabine cared so much? Trey thought dully. Probably none of his questions would ever be answered. He'd die still wondering why everything had happened, what any of his bravery had been worth.

Nedley put the truck in park and sprang out of the driver's seat.

"Don't just stand there—help me load," he hissed at Trey.

Trey glanced from Nedley to the warden, rushing toward him. He didn't really make a choice. He still had no hope of escape, but why confront his doom any sooner than he had to?

Trey crammed the fax into his pocket. Then, with Nedley's help, he hoisted Nina, Lee, Joel, John, and the chauffeur onto the truck. Out of the corner of his eye, Trey could see the warden, huffing furiously, and two guards marching up behind him.

Of course. The warden wouldn't do anything as undignified as grabbing Trey himself. He'd have someone else do the dirty work for him.

"You climb in too," Nedley whispered to Trey.

"Huh?" Trey said.

In answer, Nedley shoved Trey, knocking him forward into the open truck bed. Nedley half-fell, half-climbed in on top of him.

"Stop! Wait! My hand's caught in the chain!" Nedley called out loudly.

As if that were a cue, the truck suddenly jerked forward. Frantically, Trey clutched at the chains to keep from falling out the back. Nedley yanked up on the liftgate, trapping them all in the truck bed. The truck surged on, gathering speed.

"Help! The prisoner—we're being kidnapped! Wait!

Don't shoot—I'll get him!" Nedley stood up in the truck bed and began weaving toward the front of the truck, stepping over Lee and Nina and the others.

Trey wasn't sure what was happening—whose side was Nedley on? Just in case, Trey tackled him, kicked him away to the side, then dived through the open window into the cab of the truck.

Mark was in the driver's seat now, looking grim. His broken leg was covered with white plaster, from his knee down to his foot. He had the bottom of his cast jammed against the gas pedal.

"What are you doing?" Trey screamed at Mark. "Didn't you see those trucks back there? They'll catch us in nothing flat!"

"No they won't," Mark said, glancing over his shoulder anyhow. "We slashed all their tires."

"You did?" Trey marveled.

Mark weaved around a guard running toward them waving a gun.

"Pretend to hit me," Mark said. "Then lean down and push on the gas pedal as hard as you can. My leg's killing me."

Trey swung broadly at Mark, slipped down, and reached over Mark's cast for the pedal.

"Faster? Slower?" he called up to Mark.

"Faster. Always faster," Mark muttered.

Trey pushed even harder, straining the muscles in his arms. It was terrifying not to know what they were speeding toward. He remembered the high fences, the razor wire everywhere.

"The gates!" he screamed at Mark. "The guard! How are we going to get past—"

"The gates are still open for the other truck, the one from Slahood," Mark muttered. "And the guard—"

Trey heard a pinging sound off to the side.

"Well, he missed," Mark said matter-of-factly. "He just wasn't a very good aim."

Trey pushed even harder on the accelerator. Mark was swerving now, turning the steering wheel in wide arcs above Trey's head. Trey could still hear gunfire.

"I thought we were past the gates!" he yelled. "Who's shooting at us now?"

"Remember that truck from Slahood?" Mark asked, turning the wheel even more widely.

Trey heard more shots. They sounded closer than ever. But Mark just started laughing.

"What's happening?" Trey screamed. He hated not knowing, not being able to see. *If I get out of this alive,* Trey vowed, *I'm never hiding again.*

"All right!" Mark called out joyously. "That Nedley— what a guy!"

"WHAT IS GOING ON?" Trey screamed. "WHAT DID NEDLEY DO?"

"He shot out all the tires on the other truck," Mark said. "They just stopped. They've lost us now. Oh, man—we are home free!"

CHAPTER *THIRTY-TWO*

They weren't, of course. They were still miles from anyone's home. They were fugitives now, likely to be shot
on sight. And Trey still didn't know why Nedley was helping them, who the mysterious prisoner was, or why the
chauffeur had ended up in the back of their truck.

Still, after about fifteen minutes, they felt safe enough
to pull over by the side of the road and let Trey take over
all the driving responsibilities. (Trey was so happy to
finally be able to see out that he didn't mind the bright
sun in the least.) Another fifteen minutes later, Trey
steered the truck into a small copse of trees, totally hidden
from the road. He and Nedley went back and brushed the
gravel back into a normal formation, erasing all signs of
their tracks.

"Why?" Trey asked. "Why did you help me and Mark?"

"*Liber,*" Nedley breathed.

"Oo-oh," Trey said slowly. "Then there were more in the
liber club than just two."

"There were dozens of us," Nedley said.

"That's great. I mean—" Trey was trying to grasp it.

"Most of us are dead now," Nedley said. "But at least you and Mark and I have saved our leader."

"Who?" Trey said.

"The extra prisoner in the back of the truck," Nedley said. "Don't you know who that is?"

Trey shook his head. Everything had happened too fast; it wasn't like there'd been time for introductions.

"Whoever it is, are you sure he's still alive?" Trey asked.

"Let's go see," Nedley said grimly.

They trudged back to the truck. Lee and the others were just beginning to sit up, to cautiously peer over the edge of the truck bed.

"Trey?" Lee gasped, his voice cracking in astonishment.

"At your service," Trey said.

"You're wearing a Population Police uniform," Lee said.

"I told you you wouldn't believe what we had to go through to rescue you," Mark said peevishly from the front of the truck.

"But you look so . . . real," Lee said.

Trey nodded silently. He saw fear in Nina's eyes, in Joel's and John's. Their gaze flickered from Trey to Nedley, in terror. For the first time, Trey felt the full weight of the uniform he was wearing.

"Aw, Luke," Mark said. "That's no way to thank somebody who just rescued you from jail."

Lee's gaze steadied.

"I owe you," he said quietly.

"And I owe you," Trey said. He hoped there'd be time later to explain what he meant, how grateful he was to Lee for teaching him how to run, how to tackle—how to do something besides hide.

How to be brave.

"I think Mr. Talbot needs a doctor," Nina announced.

Trey stared—the extra prisoner in the truck was, indeed, Mr. Talbot. Trey hadn't recognized him before because he was so battered. Both his eyes were swollen shut and surrounded by huge purple bruises, his lip was split in several places, his breathing was shallow and raspy.

But suddenly it all made sense. Mr. Talbot had been a double agent within the Population Police. So had the *liber* group. Of course they were connected. Of course Mr. Talbot had been the *liber* leader. Jonathan Sabine must have been trying to mount a rescue mission for his leader that day back at the Talbots', and he'd mistaken Trey for another member of the group. That mistake had saved Trey's life.

But someone inside the *liber* group must have betrayed Mr. Talbot, the Sabines, and all the others who were dead now.

Nina was feeling for Mr. Talbot's pulse.

"I don't know—shouldn't his heartbeat be stronger than this?" she asked.

"Average resting adult heart rate is fifty to a hundred beats per minute," Trey said. "But an elite athlete in really good shape could have a rate as low as twenty-eight to forty."

Lee and Nina started laughing. Trey stood stunned for a minute, then realized it was hilarious he'd been able to spit that out, on cue, in the midst of everything else that was going on.

Thanks, Dad, he thought. *You really did teach me some useful information.*

Then they were all serious again. Nedley scrambled up onto the truck and felt Mr. Talbot's other wrist.

"He's not an elite athlete," Nedley said. "I don't think this is a good pulse."

"What are we supposed to do?" Nina asked.

"I know a place we can go," Nedley said. "A place where someone can take care of him. And where the rest of us will be safe. As safe as possible, anyway."

"But can we get there without being caught?" Trey asked. "And can we trust . . . everybody?" He couldn't help glaring right at the chauffeur, who had driven off and abandoned Trey back at the Talbots' house.

Nina seemed to understand what he meant.

"Trey, we didn't want to leave you behind," Nina said gently. "I—I'm so sorry I pushed you out of the car. We got scared when we saw Mr. Talbot taken away, but we were going to come back for you as soon as it was safe—we were watching through the trees. But when we saw the Population Police officer find you on the porch . . . How is it that you weren't killed?"

Trey tried to understand how it must have looked to them.

"The officer who found me was working with the resistance group," Trey said. "Just like Mr. Talbot. Just like Nedley here."

"And me," the chauffeur said. "I too had been fighting behind the scenes. Mr. Talbot had sent me to the Grants' house to keep an eye on all of you. I don't believe I did my job very well."

"It wasn't your fault that Mr. Talbot was captured," Nina said soothingly. "It wasn't your fault the Population Police took over the Grants' house."

Trey tried to understand.

"So you were working for Mr. Talbot," he said to the chauffeur. "Why didn't you tell us that after Mr. and Mrs. Grant died?"

"Would you have believed me?" the chauffeur asked.

Trey doubted that he would have. He'd felt so confused then. Everything had been in turmoil.

"I thought I could just take you to Mr. Talbot and every-thing would be all right," the chauffeur said.

The chauffeur was an adult, but Trey realized that he'd been every bit as stunned as Trey was to see the Population Police officials swarming over the Talbots' property. He'd felt every bit as helpless. And, like Trey, he'd made a few wrong choices along the way.

"We thought it was lucky that the chauffeur had seen where Lee's family lived. We thought we were saving Lee.

But when we got back to the Grants' house, the Population Police were there too," Nina said. "We were arrested for breaking and entering, just for driving through the front gates. We didn't know . . ."

"We didn't know anything," Lee said.

"We still don't," Joel muttered.

Trey had almost forgotten that the younger boy was there.

"All right, all right, enough with the rehashing," Nedley said. "We need to go to our safe place *now*. I know a back way. How about if I drive?"

Trey settled into the back of the truck with his friends, and Nedley slipped behind the wheel. He drove down a rutted path Trey never would have noticed.

Trey leaned over and whispered in Lee's ear: "What if Nedley can't be trusted? What if he's taking us into greater danger, instead of to safety?"

Lee just shrugged. There really wasn't anything they could do, not with Mark's leg broken and Mr. Talbot unconscious. And, for that matter, Lee and Nina and Joel and John and the chauffeur all looked pale and shrunken, as if they couldn't have jumped from the truck if their lives depended on it.

"Did they feed you in prison?" Trey asked.

Lee shook his head.

"Not much," he said. "Gruel once or twice. Maybe every third day."

They'd gone almost a week with barely any food at all—

no wonder they just sat and stared blankly, as if they didn't have enough energy to register the sight of the trees zip-ping past them, the branches whipping around the truck.

Trey tensed his muscles and stared ahead, ready to defend them all if need be.

But when they emerged from the trees, Trey relaxed immediately.

A large, windowless building stood directly ahead of them, like a welcoming fortress. It was one of only two places Trey had ever felt at home.

They were back at Hendricks School.

CHAPTER *THIRTY-THREE*

Nedley parked the truck in front of Mr. Hendricks's cottage. Mr. Hendricks rolled out in his wheelchair immediately. His eyes were focused on the Population Police insignia on Nedley's black shirt.

"I told you before!" he shouted. "You've already taken all my able-bodied workers. I have nothing more to—" He broke off, his glance finally taking in the rest of the truckload of people. Relief and joy played over his expression, but then he seemed to rein in his emotions, and he just stared in silence.

Of course. He didn't know what was going on or what he could safely say.

"Relax, old man," Nedley said. "I'm bringing people back to you. And everyone here can be trusted."

Then Mr. Hendricks rolled joyously forward, calling out, "Lee! Nina! Joel! John! I thought I'd never see any of you again. And—" He was looking around, looking worried. His gaze finally settled on Trey. "Trey?" he asked hesitantly. "In uniform?"

MARGARET PETERSON HADDIX

"It's a long story," Trey said.

"I have George, too," Nedley said. "But he's not in very good shape. Is your nurse still here?"

Mr. Hendricks didn't answer, just turned his head and yelled back toward the house, "Theodora! It's George!"

A woman came running out of the house—a woman with bright red hair streaming out behind her. Mrs. Talbot.

She was peering toward the cab of the truck, as if she expected Mr. Talbot to be in the driver's seat, in control. She didn't gaze into the truck bed until she'd looked everyone else in the face. She did a double take when she got to Trey.

"You!" she said. "You said you'd help me. And I—I didn't believe you. . . ."

She was crying even before she reached down and cupped Mr. Talbot's battered face in her hands. He moaned softly in his sleep.

"Somebody help me get him into the house," she commanded. "He'll need fluids, and I want to make sure there are no internal injuries."

Trey stared at her, amazed at the transformation.

"In addition to being a giant pain in everyone's neck," Mr. Hendricks chuckled, "Theodora is a very talented doctor."

"You'll need to look at my brother's leg, too," Lee said.

"And his burns," Trey said.

"I'm fine," Mark growled.

In the end, Trey, Nedley, and Mrs. Talbot worked together to carry Mr. Talbot into the house. All the others limped and hobbled in on their own. Mr. Hendricks bustled around serving vegetable broth and toast.

"You're sure nobody followed you? You couldn't be tracked here?" he muttered under his breath to Nedley.

"I don't think so," Nedley muttered back. "But who's sure of anything right now?"

Trey wasn't as hungry as the others, but when he sat down on one of Mr. Hendricks's couches, he found himself dozing off, then jerking awake as soon as the nightmares started.

"When was the last time you got any sleep, young man?" Mrs. Talbot asked.

"Sleep?" Trey said as if it was a foreign word he'd never heard before. "Um, the night before last, I guess." He'd slept on the floor of the barn, back at Mark's family's farm. It seemed several lifetimes ago.

"Go in the back bedroom then, and lie down," Mrs. Talbot said.

"But—" Trey wasn't sure he could trust himself to sleep ever again.

"Doctor's orders," Mrs. Talbot said. "You're safe now. You'll be hallucinating soon if you don't get some good sleep. And change out of that horrible uniform—it's giving me the creeps!"

Trey obeyed all of her commands, because it was easier than resisting. He lay on the bed, but every time he closed his eyes he saw a different horror: The Nezeree warden looming over him, yelling, "Give me my fax!" The mob swarming around him screaming, "Food! Food! Give us food!" The Population Police official back at the Grants' house, demanding, "Give me your I.D. card."

I don't have an identity card anymore, Trey thought. *The Nezeree warden surely knows now that I'm an enemy. How much longer before we're caught?*

Mrs. Talbot knocked on his door and came into the room holding up a white tablet and a glass of water.

"Sleeping pill," she said. "You probably need it."

"Is Mr. Talbot okay?" Trey asked.

"I'm hoping he will be," she said. "Thanks to you. I—I'm stunned. I didn't think anyone could save him."

Trey swallowed the pill.

"I didn't either," he admitted.

And then he slipped into the deepest sleep of his life, one without dreams of any kind.

When he woke up it was dark outside, and the house was quiet. And Trey was starving. He found an ordinary shirt and pants waiting at the foot of his bed, and he put them on. Then he crept out of his room and down the hall.

All his friends were clustered around the fireplace in the living room.

"I told him to go on without me, but Trey said, 'No!'" Mark was saying. "And before I could say anything else, he jumped out into the crowd and shouted, 'Gimme! Gimme! Hey, wait, some of the food rolled under the truck!' He tricked the crowd into moving the truck back on its wheels. And then, cool as a cucumber, he tricked them into running away from the truck, then picked me up, just like Superman, and—"

"You're making it sound easy," Trey objected. "You aren't telling how scared I was."

Mark turned to look at him.

"You didn't look scared to me," he said.

Is that how all heroic epics work? Trey wondered. *They only tell about the bravery and leave out the fear?*

"Have some popcorn," Lee said, but he was looking at Trey in awe.

Trey grabbed a handful.

"I want to hear about your adventure, Mark," he said. "How you and Nedley set up our escape at Nezeree."

"Oh, that," Mark said modestly. "There's not much to tell."

"Tell it anyway," Trey said.

Mark shrugged.

"My leg hurt so bad I could hardly think," he said. "I'm not sure I was even really awake when you got out of the truck. So, the next thing I know, this scary-looking Population Police officer's sitting next to me. I guess I was delirious, because I just started moaning, 'Liber, liber'— because it saved me that other time, you know? And this officer, Nedley, starts looking at me and looking at me—"

"I was scared to death you were a setup, and you were trying to trick me into betraying myself," Nedley said from the couch behind them. Trey glanced back—Nedley had also changed out of uniform into civilian clothes.

"And Nedley starts saying, 'Shut up! Quit that!' And I knew it really meant something to him. So I asked for his help," Mark said.

"Don't tell the story like that," Nedley laughed. "What he said was 'Quit pretending you're a bad guy. I need your help, and I need it now!' I was so surprised I almost drove the truck right into the infirmary wall."

"I didn't say that, did I?" Mark asked.

"Sure did," Nedley said, chuckling. "And then Mark was the one who came up with the idea to make it look like he was kidnapping everyone. He thought nobody would shoot at us if there was a chance of 'innocent' Population Police guards being hit."

"They shot at us anyway," Trey said. He stared into the fire, with its ever-changing flames.

"Well, yeah," Mark admitted. "But maybe not as much as they would have otherwise."

"So I took Mark on into the infirmary, and they set his leg and cleaned out his wounds," Nedley said. "They weren't gentle, either. They aren't, with prisoners. But then five minutes later, Mark's out hopping from truck to truck in the prison parking lot, cutting the tires. I would have laughed myself silly, watching him, if I hadn't been so scared we were going to get caught."

"I can't believe it worked," Mark said.

"I can't believe you got us *and* Mr. Talbot out of prison," Lee said.

"That was thanks to Jonas Sabine," Trey said. "He planned it all."

They were all silent then, and Trey knew that the others had heard about the Sabines.

"Jonas was a good man," Mr. Hendricks murmured softly. "He was my friend."

"Maybe they haven't executed him yet," Trey said. "Maybe they're still interrogating him—"

"No, they announced his death on TV," Mr. Hendricks said heavily. "On the regular channels. The Population Police are trying to discourage all dissent by showing what happened to Jonas. It was—it was a horrible death."

"God rest his soul," Mrs. Talbot said. "God help us all."

And somehow this was the scariest thing of all, to hear Mrs. Talbot sounding so solemn and reverent. She'd changed since the last time Trey had seen her, when she'd bragged about polishing her fingernails, when she'd smashed expensive sculpture just for spite.

I've changed, too, Trey thought. *We all have.*

But what did that mean about their futures?

CHAPTER *THIRTY-FOUR*

For a week, Trey and his friends lived like invalids. They ate, they slept, they lay around. Sometimes they watched television, but it was almost always Aldous Krakenaur making glorious speeches in front of a cheering crowd. Sometimes Trey felt feisty enough to jeer back at the screen, "Oh yeah, and what are you not showing us? How many people starved today?" Mostly they all sat in silence, trembling before Krakenaur's shouting image, until someone got up the gumption to snap the television off.

Trey knew his friends needed the time to heal and recover. Maybe he did too. He found himself reacting oddly to the bits of news that dribbled in. It was two or three days before he asked Mr. Hendricks anything about his fellow classmates at school.

"I know they wouldn't be outside making noise," Trey said. "But—they're all okay over there, aren't they?"

Mr. Hendricks sighed heavily.

"No," he said. "After the Government fell . . . after the

Population Police took over . . . they closed down all the schools. Temporarily, they said. They came and took away all my students for work camps. They took away the able-bodied teachers, too. . . ."

Trey could do nothing but stare at Mr. Hendricks in horror.

"I guess my wheelchair saved me," Mr. Hendricks said. "That and the garden Lee had all the students plant back in the spring."

And then Trey understood that everyone was gone, that the Population Police had left Mr. Hendricks behind to die. They didn't know that Mr. Hendricks had plenty of food to survive the winter—plenty, even with nine extra people around.

But Trey said nothing more to Mr. Hendricks. He just went and sat down to watch more television with Lee.

A few days later, Mrs. Talbot announced that Mr. Talbot was certain to make a full recovery.

"He's sitting up and speaking coherently," she raved. "It's a miracle."

And Trey just nodded, as numb to joy as he was to fear and pain.

That evening, Mrs. Talbot stopped Trey in the hallway outside Mr. Talbot's room.

"He wants to see you now," she said.

"M-me?" Trey stammered. "Are you sure he didn't want Lee?"

"Nope," Mrs. Talbot said, shaking her head with just a

trace of her old playfulness. "He asked for you by name."

Trey followed Mrs. Talbot into Mr. Talbot's sickroom. Mr. Talbot's bruises had turned a sickly shade of yellow, but he could open his eyes now. Where it wasn't bruised, his face looked pale even against the white pillowcase.

"I—don't remember some things," Mr. Talbot rasped. "But I remember—you came to see me that last day. You were at my door when they were already in my house, ready to take me away. Why? Why were you there? What was so . . . important?"

"The Grants," Trey said. "They—" He broke off. He couldn't tell a man who'd just barely escaped death that two of his closest friends were dead.

"Theo told me about them," Mr. Talbot said. He slumped against his pillows. "That was all?"

"No," Trey wanted to say. "We were terrified and we wanted you to take care of us. To make everything better." But he knew that wasn't possible now. Mr. Talbot wasn't the all-powerful, all-knowing operator anymore. He was a defeated, seriously injured man huddled in a bed in a tiny cottage. And if the Population Police found him now, he'd likely be killed.

"I was going to give you the papers I found in Mr. Grant's secret office," Trey said instead, with a shrug.

This news transformed Mr. Talbot. He sat up straight, as if he'd just been miraculously cured.

"You were? Do you still have them?" he asked.

Trey had transferred the papers from the truck into his

flannel shirt, then into his first Population Police uniform, then into the second one when he took a shower and changed back at Nezeree. But he hadn't really looked at them since that first day back in the limousine. He supposed they were still tucked into the uniform, along with the warden's fax, everything crumpled on the floor in his bedroom, kicked into a corner to be forgotten.

"I guess," he said.

"Can you bring them to me now?" Mr. Talbot asked eagerly.

"Sure," Trey said.

He went and got them. He smoothed out the wrinkles and fold marks and handed the papers to Mr. Talbot.

"They're just financial records," Trey said dully. "Mr. Grant owed you money when he died."

"No," Mr. Talbot said. "They're codes. Each of these numbers represents a third child with a fake I.D. Grant thought I was just running a black-market business on the side. . . . He thought we were laundering money; even he never knew the truth. But if Krakenaur had found this . . . if the Population Police had been able to decode this . . . there would have been no hope for any of us."

Trey gazed down at the documents with new respect. He remembered how he'd wanted to put them in the knapsack, which the Population Police confiscated and the mob tore apart. He remembered how he'd thought of using them to bargain with the Population Police for Mark's release. He remembered how he'd considering leaving them back at the Nezeree prison. It seemed like a miracle that he'd managed to bring them safely to Mr. Talbot.

"I brought these from *your* house," he said, holding out the rest of the papers. "And there are more out in the truck. Are these codes too?"

"No. That one's just a grocery list," Mr. Talbot said, pointing. "And this was a math worksheet my daughter did when she was a little girl. . . ." His face softened. Trey looked down at the row of numbers, with the name "Jen" written crookedly on them. "Thank you for bringing this to me," Mr. Talbot murmured.

Mrs. Talbot gazed over his shoulder, tears in her eyes. Trey felt like he was intruding on a private moment.

Maybe, back home, Mom acts this way when she comes across papers I wrote, he thought. Just because she'd sent him away, it didn't mean she didn't miss him.

It didn't mean she didn't love him.

"What are you going to do with the papers now?" Trey asked, to distract himself from the lump in his throat. "The ones with the secret codes, I mean?"

Mr. Talbot's expression turned stony again.

"Destroy them," he said. "We'll burn them in the fireplace, so there's no danger of the Population Police ever finding them."

"We can make a ceremony of it," Mrs. Talbot said. "Ceremonial defiance—I like that."

"But—," Trey said.

"But what?" Mr. Talbot said.

Trey could only shake his head. He couldn't quite figure out why he wanted to object. Except he didn't think miracles should be destroyed.

Isn't it enough to know that the Population Police won't ever get those papers? he asked himself.

Mrs. Talbot borrowed a spare wheelchair from Mr. Hendricks and wheeled Mr. Talbot out into the living room. Mr. Hendricks rounded up everyone else. Lee lit a fire in the fireplace.

Mrs. Talbot held the papers high over her head.

"Aldous Krakenaur, eat your heart out," she proclaimed gleefully. "Here are one hundred children who are safe from you forever."

"Nobody will ever know who they are," Mr. Talbot intoned solemnly from his wheelchair.

Trey watched Mrs. Talbot lower the papers toward the flames. The words *Nobody will ever know who they are,* echoed in his head.

"Yes they will," he muttered to himself.

Mrs. Talbot gently placed the first page in the fire. The flames began to lick at the edges. In seconds, the codes would be nothing but ash.

Trey sprang up from the couch and grabbed the paper out of the fireplace. The flames continued to eat away at the edges, hungrily working toward the all-important numbers in the center of the page, hungrily working toward Trey's fingers. He dropped the paper to the carpet and stomped out the fire.

Everyone was staring at him, speechlessly. Mrs. Talbot, who'd been about to put the next page in the fire, stood frozen, her arm stopped mid-reach.

"*They'll* know," Trey said. "The kids will. Even if every trace of their old identities—every paper record—is destroyed, they'll still know who they are. Lee, who are you? Really?"

"I'm—" Lee began, and stopped.

Mark finished for him.

"He's Luke Garner," Mark said. "And even if he spends the next fifty years pretending to be Lee Grant, he'll still be Luke Garner. My brother."

He thumped his cast on the floor for emphasis.

"And you, Nina," Trey said. "Do you think of yourself as Nina? Or—"

"Elodie," Nina whispered. "Underneath it all, I'm still Elodie."

"And Joel and John, you've gotten new fake names *twice.* Do you still remember who you began as?"

Silently, as timid as mice, the two younger boys nodded.

"And *I*," Trey said, "am *not* Travis Jackson. I'm braver than I used to be, I've done things now that I never would have dreamed of before. But I'm still Trahern Cromwell Torrance. I always will be."

It was terrifying and thrilling, all at once, to say his name aloud. Trey turned to address the grown-ups.

"Don't you see?" he said. "You've been wonderful helpers, but you don't know what it's like to be a third child. An illegal. The Population Police want to destroy us, to erase us from the earth. But—" He grabbed the remaining papers from Mrs. Talbot's hands and shook them. "If anyone can defeat the Population Police, it's us. It's our lives at stake. We need these names, so we can unite all the third children. So we can resist their evil. Together."

A stunned silence filled the room, then Mr. Talbot muttered sadly, "He sounds just like Jen."

Trey remembered that Jen and her friends had died in their quest for freedom.

Somehow that fact didn't scare him now.

Mr. Hendricks cleared his throat.

"Trey, I admire your sentiment," he said. "Truly I do. And your courage. You've already accomplished an incredible feat, saving your friends. But the Population Police have taken over everything now. George here spent years assembling his resistance movement, and it's all gone now; I fear that the only ones left are in this room tonight. So, your little speech was certainly impassioned and noble—but not very realistic."

"The game is *over*," Mrs. Talbot said. "We lost."

Trey looked from face to face, trying to gauge the emotions of his friends and the adults he'd grown to admire. These were the bravest people he'd ever met. But they all looked terrified.

"So what are you going to do?" he asked. "Hide out here forever?"

"What else can we do?" Mr. Hendricks asked.

They did mean to keep hiding, he realized. After everything that had happened, the most they felt capable of was to huddle in an out-of-the-way cottage and pray they were never discovered.

"I, for one, have had enough of hiding," Trey said, amazed at the words he heard coming out of his own mouth. But they were true. "The Population Police are not invincible. They have mobs attacking them." He remembered the sentry on the bridge. "Their own officers desert and steal their food. With all those televised speeches and cheering crowds, Aldous Krakenaur would have you believe that he's wildly popular and totally in control. But he hasn't consolidated his power. His organization is . . . disorganized. He's vulnerable *now*. If we hide out and wait and bide our time, maybe we'll miss the biggest chance of our lifetimes."

"Again, pretty words," Mr. Hendricks said. He had an edge to his voice now. "But what do you propose to *do*?"

Trey didn't know. He felt like he'd talked himself out onto a limb, and was about to fall flat on his face. Maybe his words were just words after all; maybe they were meaningless.

And then, he did know what he had to do.

"I joined the Population Police," he said. "I can go back. I can watch and listen and . . . and sabotage them. Like Mr. Talbot did. And I can find others to help me."

"You'd be gambling that we managed to fool the warden back at Nezeree," Nedley said. "And that there's not a price out on your head because of your connection to the Sabines."

"I can join again under another identity. In disguise. Nobody paid any attention to me as Travis Jackson except the warden. I'd just have to avoid him and Nezeree. I *can* get another identity, can't I?" Trey directed this question at Mr. Hendricks.

After a brief pause, Mr. Hendricks nodded.

"It's a hard life," Mr. Talbot said. "Dangerous. The most likely outcome is death."

He stared into the fire, and Trey knew that he wasn't just watching the flames. He was remembering all his friends and trusted colleagues, now dead. He had been beaten nearly to death himself.

"I know," Trey said. "But I have to try. Will—" He swallowed hard. "Will anyone come with me?"

The question hung in the air like smoke, and for a moment Trey feared that no one would answer it. He didn't want to go alone. But he would if he had to.

Then Nedley stepped forward.

"I'm in," he said. "I'm not much for waiting around; I'm ready for another adventure. If it's the death of me, so be it."

Lee was nodding too.

"Being in prison scared me," he said. "Some things are . . . worse than death. But I stood back and let a friend be the brave one once before. This time, I'm going with Trey."

"Me too," Nina said.

"And me," the chauffeur said.

Everyone looked at Joel and John, who silently shook their heads.

"You can wait, and maybe join up later," Trey said gently. Who was he to shame anyone else for cowardice?

"Wait a minute," Mark said. "What about me?"

Trey had almost forgotten Mark.

"This isn't your cause," Trey said. "It doesn't have to be. You can go home and not worry—"

"No." Mark was shaking his head violently. "You said all those third kids remember who they really are—don't you think their families remember too? Don't you think their families agonize and worry and fret, every day their kid is away? Every day of the kid's life? My brother's gone off without me twice already. Not again. I'll take the truck back home and let my leg and burns heal and then—wherever you need me, that's where I'll be."

Trey looked back at the grown-ups.

"We'll do anything we can for you," Mr. Hendricks said. "In the background. That's—that's the best we can do."

He had tears in his eyes, but Trey couldn't tell if they were tears of regret or fear. Or maybe sorrow. Maybe he was already mourning Trey and his friends.

Mrs. Talbot handed Trey the rest of the papers.

"You are responsible now for one hundred lives," she said.

"I know," Trey said.

He felt the full weight of the burden. He'd taken on the

responsibility of rescuing Mr. Talbot and Lee and the others, and that had felt too heavy. He'd messed up again and again and again—being discovered on Mr. Talbot's porch, rattling the weights in the Talbots' basement, leaving the knapsack behind in the woods, crashing through the heat ducts, killing the truck's engine right when the mob attacked. But everything had worked out in the end. Somehow, against all reason, he had faith that he could handle this responsibility as well.

With help.

CHAPTER *THIRTY-FIVE*

T rey stood at the back of a long line of men and boys. Papers rustled under his shirt—dangerous papers, papers that could get lots of people killed. And he was waiting to walk into Population Police headquarters, the most dangerous place in the country for third children.

But he waited patiently, unfazed by the sun beating down on his head, the sullen crowd around him. His friend Lee stood by his side. And his friends Nina, Nedley, and the chauffeur were already inside.

Trey glanced over at a Population Police officer leaning lazily against a tree, watching the line.

"You don't know what's going to happen," Trey wanted to tell the officer. "The only reason you can stand there so carelessly is that you don't know what we're about to do."

Trey didn't know everything either, of course. But for once in his life, he felt brave enough to face it all.